SCORNED BY
THE BOSS

MAUREEN
CHILD

Silhouette®

Desire

Published by Silhouette Books
America's Publisher of Contemporary Romance

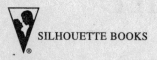

SILHOUETTE BOOKS

ISBN-13: 978-0-373-76816-5
ISBN-10: 0-373-76816-8

SCORNED BY THE BOSS

Recent books by Maureen Child

Silhouette Desire

Society-Page Seduction #1639
*The Tempting Mrs. Reilly #1652
*Whatever Reilly Wants #1658
*The Last Reilly Standing #1664
**Expecting Lonergan's Baby #1719
**Strictly Lonergan's Business #1724
**Satisfying Lonergan's Honor #1730
The Part-Time Wife #1755
Beyond the Boardroom #1765
Thirty Day Affair #1785
†Scorned by the Boss #1816

Silhouette Nocturne

‡Eternally #4
‡Nevermore #10

*Three-Way Wager
**Summer of Secrets
‡The Guardians
†Reasons for Revenge

MAUREEN CHILD

is a California native who loves to travel. Every chance they get, she and her husband are taking off on another research trip. The author of more than sixty books, Maureen loves a happy ending and still swears that she has the best job in the world. She lives in Southern California with her husband, two children and a golden retriever with delusions of grandeur.

You can contact Maureen via her Web site www.maureenchild.com.

To friendship. That amazing, wonderful sense of belonging you can only find with someone who knows the real you and loves you anyway.

And to my friends, thanks for everything.

One

Caitlyn Monroe knocked once, then entered the lion's den.

She was prepared, like any good lion trainer, for whatever might be waiting for her. A furious, chained beast looking for something to chew on? Probably. A pussycat? Not likely. In the three years she'd worked for Jefferson Lyon she'd learned that the man was much more likely to be snarly and aggressive than accommodating.

Jefferson was used to getting his own way. In fact, he accepted nothing less. Which was what made him both an amazingly successful businessman and a sometimes pain-in-the-neck boss.

But this she was used to. Dealing with Jefferson's demands was normal. And after the jolt she'd had over the weekend, she was ready for the normal. The everyday. The routine. She appreciated the fact that she knew Jefferson Lyon. Knew what to expect and wouldn't be blindsided by something shattering coming out of nowhere.

No, thanks, she thought. She'd had enough of that Saturday night.

Her boss looked up when she entered, and just for a minute, Caitlyn allowed herself to appreciate the view. Jefferson's jaw was strong and square, his blue eyes piercing enough to see through any attempts at deception and his tawny hair cut and styled to lay fashionably at his collar. A modern-day pirate with less conscience, when it came to business, than Bluebeard.

Most of the people who worked for him walked a wide berth around the magnate. Just the sound of him coming down the halls was usually enough to send people scattering. He had the reputation of being a hard man. Not always fair about it, either. He didn't suffer fools easily and expected—demanded—perfection.

So far, Caitlyn had been able to provide it. She ran his office and most of his life with proficiency. As Jefferson Lyon's personal assistant, she was expected to hold her ground against his overpowering personality. Before she had come to work here, the man had gone through assistants every couple of months. But Caitlyn was the youngest of five children in her family and she was more than used to speaking up and making herself heard.

"What is it?" he snapped and lowered his gaze back to the sheaf of files strewn across his wide mahogany desk.

Situation normal, Caitlyn thought as she let her gaze slide around the huge office. The walls were painted a deep twilight-blue, and several paintings of Lyon ships at sea dotted the wide expanse. There were two plush leather sofas facing each other in front of a gas fireplace that was cold now and a conference table sat beside a wet bar on the other side of the room. Behind Jefferson's desk, floor-to-ceiling windows provided a gorgeous view of the harbor.

"And good morning to you, too," she said, not put off by the attitude. God knows she'd had plenty of time to adjust to it.

When she'd first started working for him, Caitlyn had foolishly thought that as his assistant, she would be sort of his partner. That they would have a working relationship that would be more than his issuing orders and her leaping to fulfill them.

Hadn't taken long to disabuse her of *that* notion.

Jefferson didn't have partners. He had employees. Thousands of them. And Caitlyn was simply one of the crowd. Still, it was a good job and she was good at it. Besides, she knew he'd be lost without her, even if *he* wasn't consciously aware of that little fact.

Walking across the room, she laid a single sheet of paper down on top of the files and waited for him to pick it up and study it. "Your attorneys faxed over the numbers on the Morgan shipping line. They say it looks like a good deal."

He glanced at her again and she saw a flash of interest. "I decide what looks like a good deal," he reminded her.

"Right." She bit her lip to keep from saying that if he hadn't wanted his attorneys' opinion, then why ask for it? It wouldn't do any good, and frankly, he wouldn't want to hear it. Jefferson Lyon made his own rules. He would listen to some opinions, true, but if he didn't agree with them, then he blew them off and did whatever he thought best.

She tapped the toe of her black high-heeled shoe against the plush ocean-blue carpet. While she waited, she looked past Jefferson at the sea stretching out for what seemed forever. Passenger liners vied with cargo ships at the busy harbor. Several of those cargo ships boasted the stylized bright red lion that was the Lyon shipping company's logo. Tugboats steered boats three times their size safely out to sea. Traffic streamed over the Vincent Thomas Bridge and sunlight glittered off the surface of the ocean like diamonds, winking.

Lyon Shipping operated out of San Pedro, California, right on top of one of the busiest harbors in the country. From here, Jefferson could turn around and look at his ships as they steamed in and out of the harbor. He could see the day-to-day workings on the docks— the heavy cranes, the dockworkers loading and offloading, the steady flow of ocean traffic that made him one of the most wealthy men in the world.

But Jefferson wasn't the type to turn and admire the scenery. Instead, he spent most of his time with his back to the window and his gaze fixed on spreadsheets.

"Is there something else?" he asked when she didn't leave.

She shifted her gaze to his and felt the same jolt she always did when those blue eyes of his made contact with hers. Instantly, she thought of the conversation she'd had with Peter, her now ex-fiancé, on Saturday night.

"You don't want to marry me, Cait," he said, shaking his head and pulling out his wallet. He yanked out a twenty, tossed it onto the table to pay for their drinks, then looked at her again. "It's not me you're in love with."

Caitlyn looked at him as if he'd sprouted another head. "Hello? Wearing your ring." She waved her hand at him, just in case he'd forgotten about the two-carat solitaire he'd presented her with just six months before. "Who else do you think I'm interested in marrying?"

Peter blew out a breath. "Isn't it obvious? Every time we're together, all you do is talk about Jefferson Lyon. What he did, what he said, what he's planning."

Did she, really? She hadn't actually noticed. But, even if she did, so what?

"You talk about your boss, too," Caitlyn reminded him hotly. "It's called conversation."

"No, it's not just conversation. It's him. Lyon."

"What about him?"

"You're in love with him."

"What?" Caitlyn's voice hit a shrieky sound only dogs should have been able to hear. "You're crazy."

"I don't think so," Peter said. "And I'm not going to marry someone who really wants someone else."

"Fine," Caitlyn said, tugging the diamond from her finger and laying it on the table in front of him. "Here.

You don't want to marry me? Take your ring. But don't try to blame this on me, Peter."

"You don't get it, do you?" he said, shaking his head. "You don't even see how you feel about that guy."

"He's my boss. That's all."

"Yeah?" Peter scooted out of the booth and stood beside the table, staring down at her. "You go right ahead thinking that, then, Cait. But just so you know, Lyon's never going to see you as anything other than his assistant. He looks at you and sees another piece of office equipment. Nothing else."

Caitlyn didn't even know what to say to that. She'd been blindsided by this whole conversation. All she'd done was tell him about Jeff's plans to buy a cruise ship and how she'd miss the trip to Portugal to check it out because of their upcoming wedding. Then Peter's whole attitude had changed and he'd launched into the unexpected calling off of a wedding she'd spent six months putting together.

Just a month off now, the invitations had gone out, the gifts were already pouring in, substantial deposits had been made to the cliffside locale in Laguna. And now it seemed she'd be canceling everything.

Why in the world would Peter think she was in love with her boss? For god's sake, Jefferson Lyon was arrogant, pushy, proud and, well, downright annoying. Was she supposed to hate her job? Would that have made life easier for Peter?

"I'm sorry it worked out like this," Peter said, and started to reach out one hand toward her. He caught *himself just in time, though, and let his hand fall back to his side. "I think we would have been good together."*

"You're wrong about me," she said, looking up at a man she'd thought to spend the rest of her life with.

"For your sake," Peter said wistfully, "I wish that were true."

Then he left, and Caitlyn was alone with a naked finger and a yawning emptiness inside her.

"Caitlyn!"

Jefferson's voice snapped at her like a rifle shot and wrenched her from her memories. "Sorry, sorry."

"Not like you to be so unfocused," he said.

"I was just…" What? she asked herself. *Are you really going to stand there and tell him that your fiancé broke up with you because he thinks you're in love with the boss? Oh, wouldn't that be a good time? Get it together, Caitlyn.*

"Just, what?" he asked, shooting her a half-interested glance as he studied the spreadsheet in front of him.

"Nothing." She wasn't going to tell him. Not about canceling the wedding. Oh, she'd have to eventually, since she'd put in for four weeks of honeymoon time. And now, sadly, she wouldn't be needing it. "I wanted to remind you—you've got a two o'clock appointment with the head of Simpson Furniture and a dinner date with Claudia."

Jefferson leaned back in his deep navy-blue leather chair, folded his hands over his midsection and said,

"Don't have time for Claudia today. Cancel it, will you? And...send her something."

Caitlyn sighed, already anticipating the conversation she'd have to have with Claudia Stevens, the latest in a long string of gorgeous models and actresses. Claudia wasn't used to men not dropping to their knees to adore her. She wanted Jefferson Lyon's complete attention and she was never going to get it.

Caitlyn had known this would be coming. The man always canceled out on his dates. Or, rather, he had *her* cancel them. To Jefferson, work always came first and his life a very slow second. In three years she'd never seen him date a woman longer than six weeks—and those that lasted that long were seriously forgiving women.

Peter was sooooo wrong about her. She could never love a man like Jefferson Lyon. There was simply no future in it.

"She won't be happy."

He gave her a brief conspiratorial smile. "Hence the gift. Think jewelry."

"Fine," she said. "Gold or silver?"

He straightened up, grabbed his pen and turned back to the sheaf of papers awaiting his attention. "Silver."

"What was I thinking?" Caitlyn muttered—because, of course, *gold* wasn't gifted until the woman in question had lasted at least three weeks. "I'll take care of it."

"I have every confidence in you," he said, but she was already leaving, walking back across the immense office. "And Caitlyn?"

She stopped, turned to look at him and noticed that

the sunlight filtering in through the shaded glass gilded his hair. Frowning at that stray thought, she said, "Yes?"

"No interruptions today. Except for the two o'clock, I don't want to be disturbed."

"Right." She walked through the door, closed it behind her and leaned back against it.

She'd made it. Made it through without once caving in to the shakes still quivering her stomach. Made it without feeling her eyes well up or her temper spike. She'd managed to hold it together and talk to Jefferson without once letting her emotions slip through.

After all, just because her fiancé had dumped her didn't mean life as she knew it was over.

Jefferson worked through the day, got most of the immediate problems taken care of and finally looked up around six. Behind him, the sun was spreading color across the sky as it slid into the ocean. He didn't take the time to admire it, though. There were still plenty of things that needed his attention. Most importantly the new bid on the passenger liner he was buying. A glance at the cover letter had him wincing and stretching out one hand to hit the buzzer on the intercom.

"Caitlyn, I need to see you."

She opened the door a minute later, her purse slung over her shoulder as if he'd caught her on her way out. "What is it?"

"This," he said, standing up and walking across the room. He held out the paper to her and said, "Read the second paragraph."

Jefferson watched her tuck a strand of dark blond hair behind one ear as she read the document. And he saw her expression change slightly as soon as she caught the error he'd found only moments ago. This wasn't like her. The best assistant he'd ever had, Caitlyn simply didn't make mistakes. It was one of the reasons they did so well together.

His world ran smoothly, just the way he wanted it to. No surprises. No jolts. Everything neatly laid out in a pattern *he* chose. For Caitlyn to suddenly start making errors sent unexpected ripples through his universe.

"I'll fix it immediately," she said, lifting her gaze to his.

"Good. But what concerns me most is that the mistake happened in the first place." He jabbed his index finger at the line that had caught his attention. "Offering five hundred million dollars for the cruise ship I've already agreed to pay fifty million for is not acceptable."

She blew out a breath that ruffled the dark blond hair over her big brown eyes. "I know. But, Jefferson, no one saw this but you. It's not as if the offer actually went out this way."

"It could have."

"But it didn't."

He folded his arms across his chest and looked down at her. Even in her high heels, she came in a good five inches shorter than his own six feet two inches. "This isn't like you."

She sighed again and admitted, "I didn't type this up. Georgia did."

Impatience lit a fire in his belly. He was a man who

expected the same perfection from his employees as he did from himself. And as his admin, Caitlyn was responsible for the paperwork generated from this office. The fact that she was subcontracting to the secretaries irritated him.

"And why was Georgia involved at all? The woman is just barely competent." An older woman, Georgia Morris had been with his family's company for twenty years. She was practically an institution at Lyon Shipping. But that didn't mean that Jefferson was blind to the woman's ineptitude.

He was all for loyalty, but he had his limits.

Instantly, though, Caitlyn went on the defensive. Her posture straightened up and her chin rose to a defiant tilt. "Georgia's perfectly competent. She works hard. This was a simple mistake."

"Worth four hundred and fifty million dollars."

She winced. "She was trying to help me out."

"And why do you suddenly need help in doing a job you've performed for two years?"

"Three."

"What?"

"Three years," she said on a huff. "I've worked for you for three years."

He hadn't realized that. But at the same time, it was as if she'd always been there. A part of his day. An integral part of his business.

"Even more of a reason you shouldn't require assistance," Jefferson said, baffled at the way her eyes were beginning to flash. What in hell did she have to be upset about?

As if she'd read his mind, she took a moment and deliberately tried to calm herself. A long, deep breath, a tightening of her jaw and a long exhalation passed before she spoke again.

"I was having a hard day," she finally said. "Georgia was being nice."

"Nice doesn't get the work done," Jefferson said tightly. He had no interest in why Caitlyn had been having a "hard day." He didn't get involved in his employees' personal lives. Made for a quagmire in the office. Better that everyone kept their personal lives *personal*.

"No surprise there," she muttered.

"What?"

"Nothing."

He scowled at her. "And if you're still planning on having Georgia take over for you while you're on your honeymoon, think again. Arrange with a temp agency to send someone here who'll be able to get the job done without costly mistakes."

"That won't be necessary," she said, slinging her purse off her shoulder and heading for her desk.

Jefferson laughed shortly and followed her. "It's very necessary. You'll be gone four weeks, and Georgia running this office is unacceptable—not to mention impossible."

"No," Caitlyn said as she pulled out her desk chair and booted up her computer. "What I meant was, it won't be necessary to call a temp agency. I won't be leaving, after all."

Frowning, Jefferson walked around her desk, watching her as she set the cover letter down and prepared to retype it. It was only then he noticed that the diamond she'd worn for the last six months was missing from her left hand. This then was the reason for the hard day.

Damn it.

He scrubbed one hand across the back of his neck. He didn't want to know about her personal life. He preferred keeping business *business.* If she hadn't asked for four weeks off for a honeymoon, he might never have known that Caitlyn was getting married at all.

And now it seemed that not only wasn't the wedding happening but now that she'd brought it up, he was going to be forced into talking about it.

"What happened to the honeymoon?"

"Can't have one without a wedding," she quipped brightly, but managed to avoid looking up at him.

What was one supposed to say at a time like this anyway? Sorry? Congratulations? That would be more to his way of thinking. Why anyone would want to get married and link themselves forever to one human being who would no doubt batter them with complaints and whining for the rest of their lives was beyond Jefferson.

Still, better not to offer those particular thoughts. "So it's off."

"That would be a yes," she said, and clicked her mouse to open the word-processing program on her computer.

Apparently he'd been wrong. She had no more interest in talking about her ex than he had in listening to it. God knew that made his life easier. Yet, he couldn't help wondering why she wasn't eager to discuss it in detail.

In his experience, females liked nothing better than boring men into comas discussing their feelings, their needs, their desires, their complaints. Clearly, Caitlyn was an exception to that rule.

One eyebrow lifting, he watched as her small, efficient hands moved over the keyboard like a concert pianist's. Smooth, fast, she was finished in moments and hitting the print button. As a fresh sheet of paper slid from the printer, she reached over, plucked it up and handed it to him.

"There. Crisis averted."

He studied it briefly, nodded at the change made, then looked at her again. Whatever the reason behind the cancellation of her wedding, she seemed to be handling it well. For which he was grateful. He didn't want a weeping woman hanging about the office. He wanted his life, his world to travel on in the same way it always had. Seamlessly.

"Thanks."

She nodded, turned off the computer and gathered up her purse again. "If that's all, I'm taking off."

"Fine," he said, stepping back, already headed back for his office. Then something occurred to him and he stopped on the threshold and looked at her. "Since you're not getting married, after all, I'm assuming you'll be available for the trip to Portugal."

"What?"

Walking into his office, Jefferson kept talking, assuming—rightly—that she would be following after him. "We leave in three weeks. I want to check out the new cruise ship in person. I'll need you there with me. And since your plans have changed, I see no reason why you shouldn't be there."

He sat behind his desk, set the new cover letter atop the official offer and leaned back in his chair as she approached. His gaze narrowed as he noticed the flash of fire in her eyes and the tight slash of her mouth.

"That's it?" she said. "That's all you've got to say."

"About what?"

"About my not getting married."

"What more should I say?"

"Oh," she countered, "nothing at all." But her tone clearly indicated she'd expected something more.

"If you're looking for my condolences, fine. You have them."

"Wow." She slapped one hand to her chest and widened her eyes in feigned shock. "That was just so heartfelt, Jefferson. Wait just a minute while I catch my breath."

"I beg your pardon?" Standing up now, he faced her and watched as thoughts, emotions churned across the surface of her eyes. In the years they had worked together Caitlyn had never become emotional. Sarcastic, yes. But she'd kept their relationship as businesslike as he had. Until just this moment.

"You're not sorry at all. You're just glad that I'll be at your beck and call."

"You're always at my beck and call," he pointed out, not sure exactly where the anger was coming from.

"Oh, for god's sake. I am, aren't I?" she asked, staring at him as though she'd never seen him before.

"Why wouldn't you be?" Straightening up, he laid both hands atop his desk.

"You're right," she said. "That's my job. And I'm good at it. Too good, probably, which is why this is so twisted and messed up now. But Peter was so wrong."

"Peter? Who's Peter?"

"My fiancé." She shot him a withering glance. "My god, I was engaged to the man for six months and you didn't even know his name."

"Why would I know the damned man's name?" Jefferson asked, shoving his hands into his slacks pockets. This conversation was taking a turn he didn't care for.

"Because," she pointed out, glaring at him, "in *human* cultures, it's considered normal behavior to be interested in your fellow workers."

He snorted. "You're not a fellow worker," he pointed out. "You're my employee."

She stared at him, dumbfounded. "And that's it?"

"What more is there?"

"You know," Caitlyn snapped, tugging at the purse strap hitched over her shoulder, "I really believe you actually mean that. You have no clue. None whatsoever."

"About *what?*"

"If you don't know, I couldn't possibly explain it to you."

"Aah, the last resort of the cornered female," he said, shaking his head now. "I expected better of you, Caitlyn."

"And I expected…" She stopped, blew out a hard

breath that puffed her bangs up off her forehead so that he was treated to another peek at the dangerous sparks shooting in her eyes. "I don't know why I expected anything different. So you know what? Never mind."

"Excellent idea," Jefferson said, grabbing the opportunity to end this discussion as quickly as possible. For whatever reason, his steady, dependable assistant had slipped off her mental track. "We'll forget this conversation ever took place."

"You will, too, won't you?" Caitlyn tightened her grip on the strap of her purse, turned and headed for the door. "Well, I won't be forgetting anytime soon, Jefferson."

She was gone a moment later and he was left with irritation pulsing inside. He wasn't accustomed to *anyone* walking out on him. And he didn't like it.

Two

"Men suck." Disgusted, Debbie Harris lifted her appletini high.

"Hear, hear!" Janine Shaker picked up her Cosmo and held it poised for a toast.

"Preaching to the choir," Caitlyn said, and lifted her glass to clink against the rims of her friends' glasses. Then she took a long sip of her raspberry martini and blew out a breath.

After the weekend she'd had, not to mention that last conversation with Jefferson, it was good to be with her friends. Women who understood. Women she could count on, no matter what.

"Are you okay, honey?" Debbie asked, always the

one with the biggest heart and the soul most easily bruised. "I mean, really okay?"

"I'm fine," Caitlyn said, and surprised herself with the truth of the statement. Good god. She'd been poised to marry Peter, for heaven's sake. Shouldn't she be in mourning? Shouldn't she be weeping miserably in a corner somewhere?

Sure, she'd done some crying over the weekend, but if Peter really had been the love of her life, then wouldn't she be feeling more…shattered? But she didn't. And somehow that was even sadder than the breakup of her engagement.

"I cannot believe Peter thinks you're in love with your *boss*," Janine said on a snort of laughter. "Lyon makes you nuts."

"I think Peter was just scared and needed a reason to back out of the wedding, the big weenie," Debbie said.

"Yeah, but accusing her of being in love with *Lyon?*" Janine shook her head. "That's really stretching."

At the moment, Caitlyn could hardly even think about Jefferson Lyon without gritting her teeth. In love with him? Not a chance. Attracted? Sure. What red-blooded, breathing woman wouldn't be? But attraction was where it started and ended.

"Don't even get me started on Jefferson Lyon," Caitlyn muttered, and snatched a tortilla chip from the basket in the middle of the table. As she crunched down hard on it, only half pretending she was snapping her boss's neck in half, she told her friends, "When Jefferson found out the wedding was off, he just said, 'Oh, good. You can go to Portugal with me after all.' No I'm sorry, Caitlyn. Are you all right? Do you need to take some time off? Do you want me to kill the jerk for you?" She took a sip of her drink and reached for another chip. "I'm telling you, I came within a hair of quitting."

"You should've," Debbie said. "Men suck."

"Where've I heard that before?" Janine wondered aloud.

"Funny." Debbie smirked at her, then turned her gaze back on Caitlyn. "Anyway, Peter obviously had some commitment issues and was just using Lyon as a handy excuse."

"Well, it was a stupid one," Caitlyn said. She refused to think about the quick whip of something hot and delicious that usually zapped her whenever she was too close to Jefferson. That was just lust. Or not even that. Just…appreciation for a good-looking guy. That was it. She nodded. Appreciation. Attraction. Nothing else.

"Duh." Janine shook her head. "But the upside is he gave you a month to call it off. Unlike my own unlamented ex-fiancé, John, who thought three days was more than enough time."

True. Janine's ex-fiancé had left her a note, three days before their simple backyard wedding that read only, *Sorry, babe. This isn't for me.* Debbie was right, Caitlyn thought. Men really did suck.

"Did you tell your mom yet?" Debbie asked the question, already wincing in anticipation of the answer.

Yep, these friends knew her well. Knew her family.

Knew what kind of hell her mother was going to put her through for ruining her only shot at being mother of the bride.

"Yeah, that was a good time." Caitlyn closed her eyes and sighed, remembering the look of stunned shock, disappointment and frustration that clouded her mom's face just yesterday when she'd dropped by her parents' house to deliver the blow.

"Guessing she didn't take it well?" Janine asked.

"You could say that. You would have thought I'd… No, I can't even think of anything that could rival how this news hit Mom. She's had her dress for the wedding since the week after Peter proposed," she reminded them unnecessarily. "'Four times,' she told me yesterday, 'four times I was mother of the groom. It was my turn to be Mother Of The Bride.'"

"Yikes," Debbie muttered.

"That about covers it," Caitlyn said. "She even says the words *Mother Of The Bride* in capital letters. She's been so enjoying being in on everything. Heck, the only way I got to pick my own site was because Peter and I were paying for the wedding ourselves. Otherwise mom would have found a cathedral or something. She really was looking forward to a big show. I was her only shot at the brass ring."

"She's gonna make you pay."

Janine grumbled, "She should be making Peter pay."

"Doesn't matter," Caitlyn said with a shake of her head. "The point is it's over. And now our little circle of dumpdom is complete."

Debbie looked at her across the table. "I just can't believe *Peter* turned out to be a stinker. He seemed so nice."

Janine finished the last of her drink and scowled down at the empty glass. "They all seemed nice, at first. Mike was great to you until you found out about the other two wives he already had."

It was Caitlyn's turn to wince now. Six months ago Debbie had been within a couple of weeks of her own wedding, a planned elopement to Vegas, when she intercepted a phone call for her fiancé, Mike, at his place. Turned out that the woman on the line was Mike's wife. And by the time it all got sorted out, yet another wife had been discovered. And now Mike was in jail, where every good bigamist should land.

"True," Debbie mused, and rubbed the empty spot on her ring finger where her antique moonstone had shone brightly up until six months ago. Then she shrugged and looked at Janine. "You were in the worst shape of all of us. Only three days to cancel everything."

Janine nodded. "John always did have a flair for the dramatic. The creep."

"It's been a pretty rotten year, hasn't it?" Debbie flipped her long blond hair back over her shoulder and looked from Janine to Caitlyn. "Romance wise, I mean."

"Fair to say." Janine signaled the waitress by holding up her nearly empty glass. "What're the odds that all three of us would get engaged and then *un*engaged in the same year?"

"There's a cosmic kind of symmetry in it, I admit,"

Caitlyn said on a sigh. Running the tips of her fingers through the water mark her glass had left on the glossy tabletop, she added, "At least we have each other."

"Thank god." Janine's brown eyes narrowed as she chewed on the end of a swizzle stick.

Caitlyn took another drink of raspberry-flavored liquor and licked a stray drop off her bottom lip. "All three of us engaged, then dumped. What does that say about us?"

"That we're too good for the available men around here?" Janine offered, grinning.

"Well, sure, that," Debbie said with a smile. "But it also says here we are. Monday night and we're at the same table in the same bar where we've been meeting for the last five years."

"Hey, I like On The Pier," Janine said, signaling again to the waitress by holding up her empty glass.

"We all do," Caitlyn threw in, draining her martini to be ready for the second round already on its way. Idly she glanced across the crowded room. There were a few suits, men fresh from work, stopping by to have a quick drink on the way home. But, mostly, the crowd was made up of people like Caitlyn and her friends— relaxed, in jeans and T-shirts, looking to unwind in a comfortable spot.

On The Pier, a tiny neighborhood bar in Long Beach, had been their designated meeting place since they'd all turned twenty-one. Every Monday night, no matter what, the three women had a standing date for drinks and gossip.

And over the last year, as they'd taken turns commis-

erating with each other over broken engagements, these
Monday-night get-togethers had become more important than ever. Caitlyn ran her fingertip around the rim
of her glass and studied her two friends thoughtfully.
She found herself smiling in spite of the heavy, cold
lump settled in the pit of her stomach. The three of them
had been friends since high school, when they'd met in
detention hall.

Raised with four older brothers, Caitlyn had been
hungry for a sister. And with Debbie and Janine she'd
found two. They were closer to her than anyone else she
knew. "It's a great neighborhood bar and we know ev-
erybody here. It's our comfort zone."

"Exactly!" Debbie gulped the last of her drink and
set her glass down. Leaning her elbows on the table in
front of her, she glanced at each of her friends and said,
"That's my point. We're all in a comfort zone. We each
got dumped and we're still here. Same spot. Same day.
Same time."

"So?" Janine paused when their waitress delivered
their fresh drinks and took away the empty glasses.

When the waitress had gone, Debbie grabbed hers
and took a quick gulp of the pale green liquor. "*So,* why
are we content to stay in a comfort zone? Why don't we
break loose? Try something new?"

Caitlyn frowned at her. "Like what?"

"Like…" Debbie paused. "I don't know offhand. But
we should do something."

"Maybe—" Janine said, then quickly closed her
mouth and shook her head. "Nope. Never mind."

"What?"

"No way do you get to say that and then stop," Caitlyn protested.

"Fine." Janine grinned at each of them, then took a sip of her drink. "I've been thinking about this for a couple of days now. None of us got married. None of us got the honeymoon we were planning on. And none of us has spent the money we had been saving up for the whole wedding/honeymoon extravaganza."

"And…" Debbie prompted.

"And," Janine said, "last night it suddenly occurred to me—why don't we spend that money together?"

"How?" Caitlyn asked, intrigued enough to listen.

"On a blowout no-holds-barred vacation," Janine said, clearly warming up to her own idea as she spoke. Her eyes flashed and her grin spread. "I say we each take the four weeks' time we were going to use for our honeymoons and go on a trip together. We go to some fabulous resort, get waited on, drink, play and get laid as often as humanly possible."

"You've been thinking about this, haven't you?" Debbie said.

"Well, yeah," Janine allowed. "Since Saturday night, when Caitlyn called to tell us about Peter. Really pissed me off. And then I realized that all three of us have had a crappy year. Seems like we owe ourselves a good time."

Debbie blew out a breath, took a gulp of her drink, then set the glass down on the table. "It does sound good."

Caitlyn's blood was humming. She felt excitement stir.

She'd had a rotten weekend, a lousy day. And didn't she deserve to have a little fun? This might be just the ticket. Nodding, she said, "It's a great idea. When do we go?"

Janine looked at the two of them and laughed. "Two weeks. Enough time to get someone to cover for us at work and not so long that we'll convince ourselves not to go."

"She's right, Caitlyn. If we don't do it now," Debbie cautioned, "we'll talk ourselves out of it."

"Good point," Caitlyn said, knowing that *she* at least would second-guess the whole "fun" principle until she had convinced herself to save the money and go to work like a good girl. "Okay, then, two weeks. If we can get reservations."

"Uh, hello? Reservations where?" Debbie asked.

The voices in the bar blurred into a soft background noise, mixed with a slow song drifting from the old juke-box in a corner. Outside, a cold ocean wind rattled against the glass, but inside, Janine's eyes were flashing as she leaned across the table and whispered, *"Fantasies."*

"Whoa." Debbie slouched back in her chair.

"Really?" Caitlyn grabbed her drink and began to consider the possibilities, hardly listening as Janine kept talking. Fantasies was one of the most exclusive, indulgent resort islands in the world. Everything Caitlyn had read about the place suggested wild nights and glorious days filled with romance and pampering.

Just what the three of them needed.

"We'll never be able to get reservations there," Debbie protested.

"Already have 'em," Janine said with a wink. "I called

yesterday and put a deposit down on three rooms. They'd had a few cancellations, so we got lucky. I think it's fate's way of telling us this is our time. We need to do it."

"I can't believe you've already got the rooms."

"Well," Janine said, "I figured if I couldn't talk you guys into it, I could always cancel the reservations."

A bubble of excitement rose inside Caitlyn and she reached for it greedily. Fantasies. She'd read so much about the place in magazines and celebrity gossip columns, how could she refuse to go in person with her two closest friends? Slapping one hand on the center of the table, she said, "I'm in."

"Well, we already know I'm in, since it was my idea." Janine covered Caitlyn's hand with her own and then both of them turned to look at Debbie.

"This is crazy—you guys know that, right? I mean, we're just taking off and blowing a ton of money on a few weeks at a resort on a total whim." Debbie chewed at her bottom lip, looking from one friend to the other and back again.

"What's your point?" Janine asked.

"Don't have one," Debbie said, and laid her hand on top of her friends'. "I was just saying. Anyway, I'm in, too."

"This is gonna be great," Caitlyn said, and leaned back in her chair. "I so need this. We *all* need to get away for a while."

"Some of us more than others," Debbie muttered, and nodded in the direction of the door.

"What's he doing here?" Janine whispered.

Curious, Caitlyn turned in her seat and felt her stomach drop to her toes. Jefferson Lyon walked into the bar as if he owned the place. He stood like a well-dressed statue, his sharp blue eyes scraping the crowd until he found her. Then his gaze narrowed and he headed toward her like a man on a mission.

"Wow," Debbie whispered. "I never would have guessed he'd come to a place like this."

"Yeah," Janine said, "definitely not his style."

Caitlyn had to agree. In a crowd of blue jeans and board shorts, his Armani suit stood out like a flashing neon light. Of course, Jefferson Lyon stood out in any crowd. He just had that kind of aura. All powerful and sexy and—

Cut that thought off at the pass, she told herself firmly as she stood up to meet him. Just as she told herself that the quick spurt of something hot and heavy moving through her bloodstream was simple surprise at seeing him here.

Heck, she hadn't even known he'd been aware of On The Pier's existence.

Her gaze locked on him, but she was also aware of how every female in the room watched him move with open admiration. And how could she blame them? He had a way of walking that suggested both power and languor. He moved like a man who knew how to take charge, but liked to take his time about it. Which, of course, only made a woman wonder what that kind of mixture would be like in bed.

Oh, boy.

"Caitlyn," he said when he was close enough to be heard over the muttering crowd.

"Jefferson, what are you doing here?" Her voice came out a little sharper than she'd planned.

One eyebrow lifted. "I needed to see you about something that couldn't wait, obviously."

"How'd you know where I'd be?"

"It's Monday night. You're always here."

That little nugget of information staggered her. He hadn't known her fiancé's name, but he knew she came to this tiny bar every Monday night? "I know I am. How did *you* know I am?"

He shrugged, glanced at her friends, then looked back into her eyes. "You must have mentioned it."

And he'd remembered?

Shaking her head, Caitlyn told herself it didn't matter how he'd found her. "So what did you want, Jefferson?"

He looked down at her friends, watching them with avid interest. Nodding, he then dismissed them entirely and shifted a look around the bar, as if unsatisfied to find himself surrounded by so many people. Taking her upper arm in a firm grip, he half steered her, half dragged her, back to the entryway, where things were a little less crowded.

Caitlyn tried not to think about the tiny spears of heat the touch of his hand sent zipping through her system. She'd clearly had one too many martinis. Once free of the main room, she pulled out of his grasp, crossed her arms over her chest and tipped her head to one side, looking up at him. "What was so important it couldn't have waited until tomorrow?"

Jefferson stared down at her and realized just how different Caitlyn looked when away from the office. He was so used to her tidy, professional appearance, seeing her with her hair down and loose around her shoulders was more distracting than he would have expected. She wore faded, worn blue jeans that clung to her body like a second skin, a scoop-necked pale blue T-shirt that showed just a hint of cleavage and sandals that displayed long, elegant toes painted fire-engine red.

Even over the combined scents filling the air he could smell her perfume, something light and flowery that she never wore in the office. This was why he preferred business relationships to be kept strictly business. He didn't want to know that Caitlyn liked red nail polish. Or that she smelled like a damn garden. Or that she had a lush figure hidden beneath the boring business suits she wore to work.

Frowning to himself, he pushed away his wandering thoughts. He hadn't come to be sociable, after all.

"My father called tonight. He needs me in Seattle tomorrow afternoon. So I'll need you in the office early to take care of a few things before I leave."

Instantly, her eyes widened. "Is your father all right?"

"He's fine," Jefferson said, somehow pleased that she had cared enough to ask. His father had officially retired as head of the company two years ago, but he'd kept a hand in ever since, unable or unwilling to let go.

Then three months ago he'd had a major heart attack and was still recuperating.

Odd, but Jefferson was only now acknowledging that Caitlyn had been the only person he'd talked to about his father's health. So much for keeping personal lives separate from work.

"Good. I'm glad." She stared at him for a long minute. "But you couldn't have called me with this information?"

He could have. Should have. But he'd come for a purpose. To remind her just who was in charge in this relationship. *He* was the boss. *He* called the shots. She thought she could stomp out of his office in some kind of female huff? Well, showing up here in person reminded her that Jefferson *always* got the last word.

Of course, he hadn't intended on hunting her down in this dinky little bar. He'd planned on driving straight to his condo in Seal Beach. But the more he'd thought about her irritated attitude, the more it had annoyed him. All he knew for sure was that she'd been in the back of his mind when he'd left the office. And for whatever reason, he'd driven to the one place he'd known he'd be able to find her.

"It's not that far out of the way for me," he said, and turned when yet another customer shoved through the front door. Irritated, Jefferson caught the door, glared at the surfer stumbling through it, then turned his gaze back to Caitlyn. She was still watching him, her brown eyes glittering with the reflected lights of the room. "Anyway…my flight out is at ten, so I'll expect to see you at six in the morning."

"Fine, I'll be there." She turned to go back to her friends.

He grabbed her arm to stop her, his fingers closing around her warm, smooth skin. Damned if he'd just stand there and let her walk away from him. Again.

But as soon as he noticed that he was liking the feel of her beneath his fingers, he let her go. Then he grabbed the door behind him, yanked it open and walked through it. Stopping on the threshold, he looked back at her, pleased he was getting the last word tonight after all. "Fine. I'll see you then."

Three

Caitlyn arrived at a quarter to six in the morning to find Jefferson already on the phone in his office. No surprise there. It wasn't unusual for him to be at work hours before everyone else. After all, with contacts and business dealings all over the world, most of his phone calls had to be made early to accommodate time changes.

He'd also left a stack of files on her desk, and after making a fresh pot of coffee, she jumped right in. It was better to keep her mind busy. Too busy to think about what she and her friends had decided to do. Because, if she started thinking about it, she just might back out.

"Which I am *not* going to do," she muttered with determination.

Behind her desk, the rising sun was just streaking

across the sky in shades of lavender and gold. The scent of freshly brewed coffee filled the air and eased the jump in the pit of her stomach. In the corner, the fax machine rang, then hummed busily as it spat several sheets of paper out into a tray.

Caitlyn walked over to pick them up, gave them a quick glance. Bids from other, smaller shipping companies hoping to be a subcontractor for Lyon Shipping. Business as usual, she thought, then carried them to her desk to staple together and tuck into a file. There was always plenty to do. She'd always loved that about the job. There was never a moment in the day where she was bored enough to watch the clock, eager to escape.

The phone rang and she reached for it. Her gaze noted that the light for line two was still on, so Jefferson wasn't available.

"Lyon Shipping."

"Well," a deep, familiar voice said. "Caitlyn, love, you're at work early this morning."

She rolled her eyes and grinned. Max Striver, President and CEO of Striver Shipping, always did the subtle-flirting thing. But he was never annoying about it. His British accent flavored his speech, and Caitlyn could hear the smile in his voice.

"Good morning, Mr. Striver. How're things in London?"

"Max, Caitlyn," the man urged. "I've asked you to call me Max. And London is a ridiculously lonely place. You should come and visit me. Make the old girl shine."

"I'll put it on my list," Caitlyn said, still smiling as

she tucked the phone between her ear and shoulder and continued shuffling the files on her desk. "Mr. Lyon's on the other line, Max. Can you hold? Or do you want him to call you back?"

"If you're willing to spend a moment or two talking to me, I'll wait."

She could work and talk, Caitlyn thought. "What will we talk about, then?"

"How about when you're going to quit working for that surly American and come to work for me?"

Caitlyn sighed. "Max, you don't really want me to work for you. You only want to deprive Mr. Lyon of my expertise."

"A little of both, actually, love," he said, and his voice dropped a notch or two.

Seriously, accents should be illegal. They did something quivery to the pit of Caitlyn's stomach even when she knew Max Striver was no more interested in having her work for him than he was in moving to Tucson.

"He works you much too hard. While I, on the other hand," Max insisted, "am a very understanding employer. Good hours, better pay and, of course…*me*."

The light on Jefferson's phone line went out and Caitlyn said, "I'll keep it in mind, Max. Meanwhile, the boss is available. Hold on for a moment?"

She put him on hold, buzzed Jefferson's phone and when he answered, said, "Max Striver on line one."

"Damnit," Jefferson muttered. "What's he want?"

"Me, working for him," she said.

"Still? You'd think he'd have gotten it through his

thick head by now that there's no way you'd leave Lyon Shipping." The grumble in his voice was clear just before he disconnected and picked up the other line.

"What is it, Max?" Jefferson leaned back in his chair and swiveled it around until he was staring out at the dock below and the ocean beyond.

"Jefferson, old friend, do I need a reason for calling?"

"Usually."

He inched forward, admiring the view. A solitary tugboat, encrusted with the Lyon Shipping logo, sailed across the harbor, a frothy whip of ripples in its wake. Longshoremen moved across the docks, driving loaders and swinging nets filled with cargo off the decks of ships.

This was Jefferson's world.

He'd learned the family business from the ground up. His father didn't believe in taking the easy way and hadn't been willing to allow his son to simply step into the executive level without knowing about the men who made this company run.

Now he ran one of the most successful shipping companies in the world and he knew how to get the best out of his employees. Hadn't he remained calm and in control during Caitlyn's emotional meltdown yesterday?

He smiled to himself as he listened to the fax machine in the outer room. Even now, Caitlyn was efficiently bringing order to chaos. Everything was as it should be. As he'd known it would be once she had had a chance to calm down.

Just as he knew that Max would never be able to

steal her away to work for Striver. Caitlyn's own sense of loyalty would prevent her from leaving him for a competitor.

"Jefferson? You still there?"

He frowned slightly as he realized he'd allowed his mind to drift away from the business at hand. And when dealing with Max Striver, it paid to keep your mind on business. "I'm here, Max. And I'm busy."

"Oh, I'm sure. I'll only keep you a minute. Just wanted to let you know I heard about your trip to Portugal."

"And…"

"And I understand that the shipyard there has come to a grinding halt due to a strike."

"It was settled last week," Jefferson said, gritting his teeth as he forced a smile into his voice. "Everything's back on schedule."

"Oh, happy to hear it."

"Yeah," Jefferson said. "I'm sure."

He and Max had been competing for years—at everything from racquetball to gross tonnage shipped. Now, with the first of the Lyon cruise ships ready to set sail in just under six weeks, Max was no doubt hoping to beat Jefferson to the prime Atlantic routes.

"As it happens, I am," Max assured him. "We can't really have a competition if your boat never gets off the dock, can we? We're going to have a month's head start on you as it is."

Jefferson picked up his sterling-silver pen, tapped it against the desktop, then tossed it down. Leaning back in his leather chair, he stared up at the ceiling and smiled. "From what I hear, you should be more interested in what's happening to your own ship."

There was a pause in which Jefferson imagined Max sitting straight up in his chair and glaring at his reflection in the mirror across from his desk. A good image.

"What do you mean?"

"Well," Jefferson said, enjoying himself more now, "my man in France tells me that the new Striver ocean liner is having some trouble keeping its chefs."

"Lies."

"Uh-huh." Grinning now, Jefferson said, "You know, if you knew how to treat employees, Max, your new chef wouldn't be on his way to Portugal right now to check out the kitchen on the new Lyon cruise ship."

"You stole him away, did you?"

"Wasn't even difficult," Jefferson admitted. "Seriously, Max, you should have offered to pay the man what he's worth."

A long moment passed before Max chuckled. Then he said, "You win this round, Jeff. But the game's not over."

When he hung up, Jefferson was still smiling. Caitlyn was busy running his office, he'd managed to one-up Max—and it wasn't even eight in the morning yet.

Caitlyn's fingers flew across the keyboard as she typed up one of several memos that would be distributed throughout the company. Amazing, really, she thought, her mind free to race even while she was busy transcribing Jefferson's pitiful penmanship.

He didn't even consider for a moment that she might

one day take Max up on his offer of a job. "There's no way you'd leave, Caitlyn," she muttered, repeating his words with a bit more snide in her tone, then adding a few more things that he was no doubt thinking but hadn't said. "You're just too reliable. You're like my trusty dog, Caitlyn. Always there. Happy to help. Grateful for a stupid pat on the *head*."

It wasn't so much that she resented the fact he wasn't worried about keeping her on as his assistant, she told herself firmly as she turned to reach for the memo as it shot out of the printer. It's that she resented the fact he *wasn't* worried about keeping her on as his assistant!

Shouldn't he be worried? Shouldn't he at least have the decency to say, I hope you never leave, Caitlyn. You're too important to me. To the company.

Right. Like that would ever happen.

She shook her head, told herself she should be flattered that her boss was so sure of her loyalty. But that just didn't work. Instead, she was really irritated that it didn't bother him at all for one of his top competitors to continually be offering her a job.

"See?" she whispered. "This is why you need to take a break. You need that trip, Caitlyn. It'll be good to get away from everything for a while. It'll be good for Jefferson Lyon to have to run this place without you for a while. Maybe then he'd show some gratitude. Maybe then he'd notice you and—"

No. What was she saying?

She wasn't trying to get him to notice her as a woman. Just as a *person*.

So, yes, she should go. Think about herself first for a change and just take off. Be adventurous.

Yet, even as she said the words, her conscience was arguing with her. There was no point in going away. She wasn't getting married, didn't have a honeymoon to go on. So surely she should stay and work. Do the responsible thing. Do the *right* thing, as she always did.

Good old Caitlyn. By-the-book, follow-the-rules Caitlyn. Don't rock the boat. Don't color outside the lines.

"God, I'm so boring." She propped her elbows on the desk and dropped her head into her hands. "Pitiful. Seriously pitiful. Twenty-six years old and I've never done a damn thing just for myself. Isn't it about time, Caitlyn?" Her voice was muffled against her hands and that was probably just as well. "Don't you owe it to yourself to get out there and see some of the world and let the world see *you?*"

Sure, it was an outrageously expensive vacation. But didn't she deserve a little pampering? Didn't she owe it to herself to relax and recharge?

"God, now I'm starting to sound like Janine." She straightened up and smiled to herself as she remembered how her friend had spent the better part of an hour convincing her and Debbie that they were doing the right thing by going to Fantasies.

"Who's Janine?"

Caitlyn jolted at the sound of Jefferson's deep voice coming from right behind her. Then she laid one hand against her galloping heart and looked up at him, shaking her head. "You know, it'd probably be easier to kill me if you just hit me over the head, rather than going for the old stop-her-heart routine."

"You knew I was here."

"You were on the phone," she pointed out.

"Not now," he said. "Didn't mean to scare you." He wasn't wearing his suit jacket. The sleeves of his pin-striped white shirt were rolled back to the elbows over tanned forearms and the collar of his shirt was gaping open behind a loosened knot in his navy-blue tie. Lean-ing one shoulder against the doorjamb, he asked again, "So. Who's Janine?"

"A friend," Caitlyn said, turning her gaze back to the stack of files on her desk. God, how much else had he heard? Had he been standing there the whole time she'd been muttering about how boring she was? Perfect. That was just perfect. "You saw her at the bar last night."

"The tiny blonde or the tall spiky-haired brunette?"

"Her hair is not spiky," Caitlyn argued, "it's tousled."

"By a Weedwacker."

She'd dismiss that one. Why the interest, though? Was he trying to be nice? Because he felt guilty about not even knowing her fiancé's name? No. That couldn't be it. Jefferson Lyon didn't do guilt. So why the friendly banter? Why not just shut himself up in his office as he did every other day? Was it the early-morning quiet of the building? With only him and her there to work?

Did it even matter?

"You weren't on long with Max," she said in a blatant attempt to change the subject.

"No." Jefferson plowed one hand through his hair.

His eyes narrowed and a muscle in his jaw twitched. "He only called to goad me about the strike in Portugal and to remind me that his ship will be ready nearly a full month before ours."

"Aah." The competitors were at it again.

Jefferson shoved both hands into his slacks pockets and said, "But at least I got to remind him that we stole his top chef. Besides, Max is still stung over losing the Franco contract to us last year."

Caitlyn smiled up at her boss. That had been a real coup. Nailing down the shipping contract for Franco Technologies had taken her and Jefferson more than six months to complete. "Well, that had to make you feel better."

One corner of his mouth lifted. "True. Still, if Striver Cruise Lines opens a full month ahead of Lyon, he's going to be able to get the prime routes."

"His first ship is smaller."

His gaze snapped to hers. "You're sure?"

"First thing I did this morning," she admitted, handing him a sheet of paper that had come through on the fax just ahead of the bid from the smaller shipping company in Germany. "The shipyard in France where Max's ship is being finalized was very helpful. I simply asked for an example of their latest work, and they were happy to send me the full specs of the cruise liner they're finishing at the moment. And ours is at least three hundred feet longer. Better built for the Atlantic routes."

He tapped the sheet of paper with the tips of his fingers and gave her a smile that lit up her insides like a flash of neon. Oh, good god. She really did need that vacation.

Getting a firm grip on clearly hysterical hormones, she shifted and turned in her chair, keeping her gaze determinedly fixed on her desk. "Is there anything else you wanted, Jefferson?"

"Yeah. Actually, I wanted to make sure you had the arrangements for the Portugal trip locked down."

Glad to have him shift back to business as usual, Caitlyn shifted on her chair, picked up a manila folder and handed it to him. "All the details are right there. The Palacio Estoril is holding your usual suite. Your pilot's notified, so the company jet will be ready whenever you are. And the meetings at the shipyard are set up. The times are all listed there and the hotel will provide a car and driver."

He idly flipped through the papers, then glanced at her as he turned to head back into his office. "Get yourself a suite, too."

"That's not necessary."

"I know that, but we may as well both be comfortable."

"No," she said, taking a deep breath and holding it just long enough to quiet the ripples in the pit of her stomach. This wasn't going to be easy. Nothing with Jefferson ever was. "That's not what I meant."

Only yesterday, she'd told him she wasn't getting married and he'd assumed she'd be available for this business trip to Portugal. Now she had to tell him she'd be taking her four weeks off, anyway. And she didn't want to be sitting down when she did it. Better to be standing on her own two feet and less at a disadvantage.

That thought clearly in mind, she stood up, walked around him to the coffeepot and refilled her cup.

"What're you talking about?"

"I won't be going with you to Portugal after all, Jefferson. I'm taking my four weeks' vacation."

He frowned and his sharp blue eyes narrowed. "You're not getting married—why do you need the time?"

"Because I put in for it and I want it."

He pushed away from the wall and stalked across the room. Stopping right beside her, he picked up the coffeepot, filled a cup for himself and took a sip before shifting a look at her. "It's not convenient right now."

Her fingers tightened on the handle of the cup. "Of course it's convenient. I put in for this time nearly six months ago. Everything's arranged."

"Things have changed."

"What things?" She still had to tip her head back to look at him, and just at that moment, she wished she stood taller than her five feet eight inches.

"You're not getting married now. Therefore, you're able to accompany me to Portugal."

"You don't need me there, Jefferson."

Those eyes of his focused on her and she felt the sheer power that shone from the man. "I decide what I need, Caitlyn. And as my assistant, your presence is required."

She swallowed hard. "Tough."

"I beg your pardon?"

Setting her coffee cup down—because her hands were shaking—Caitlyn blew out a breath and told herself that if she was ever going to stand up for herself, now was the time to start. "You heard me. I work for you, Jefferson, but I'm not your indentured servant. I put in for that vacation time. It's mine and I'm taking it."

He gave her a long, narrowed look. "Take it *after* the Portugal trip."

"No. Not this time."

Damn it, she wasn't going to cave to him. Not today.

The year before, her bags had been packed, she'd had her plane ticket to Florida in her purse along with the itinerary for the cruise she'd spent three months planning. Jefferson had called just as she'd been getting into a cab, insisting she cancel her plans and accompany him to a shipyard in France. Her cruise to the Bahamas had sailed without her and she'd spent the next two weeks taking notes and in general being Jefferson's gofer.

Granted, France wasn't exactly a hardship…though she hadn't had five minutes to herself to explore the countryside or get into Paris.

And the year before that, her long-awaited trip to Ireland had been cut short when Jefferson flew the company jet into Shannon Airport and insisted she join him for an important conference in Brazil.

So *this* time Caitlyn was sticking to her guns.

She was going on this trip with her friends, and if Jefferson Lyon didn't like it…too bad. Caitlyn felt a buzz through her system as she silently declared her own private Independence Day. No more pesky work ethic. No more putting her own wants and needs on the back burner to make sure everyone else got just what they wanted.

I am Caitlyn, hear me roar, she thought, and lifted her chin defiantly as she faced down her boss.

Four

"You're being selfish."

"*I'm* selfish?" Caitlyn repeated, completely flabbergasted that he could even say such a thing. The man who believed the world revolved around him? The man who expected everyone in his life to jump whenever he entered a room? The man who'd ruined every vacation she'd ever tried to take with his own demands? "Are you serious?"

"This isn't like you, Caitlyn," he said tightly, his voice dropping to a snarl that usually had his employees in a mad dash for the closest exit.

"No," she agreed, not even flustered by that snarl. She'd heard it too often to be dismayed by it at this late date. "It's not like me at all. That's why I'm doing it."

"That makes no sense at all," he pointed out, taking

a sip of coffee, then setting his cup down on the credenza beside hers.

"It makes perfect sense." She threw her hands high, let them drop again and did a quick about-face. Marching away from him for five or six steps, she felt fury rumbling through her, and for the first time in her life, she welcomed it. Stopping dead, she whirled around to face him and pointed her index finger at him accusingly. "You totally expect me to drop everything and do whatever you want me to do. And how can I even blame *you* for it? My whole life I've done exactly what I was supposed to."

"Admirable."

"Or weak," she countered, stalking right back to him. "My parents, my brothers, Peter, *you*. You've all steamrolled over me because I kept lying down on the street and assuming the position. Allowing you all to get away with bossing me around. Well, no more. I'm done."

"Caitlyn, you work for me." His voice was deliberately cold. Tolerant. She knew the tone. She'd heard him use it on those who were trying his very limited amount of patience. But Caitlyn wasn't going to back down.

"I tell you when you take a vacation and when your presence is required," he said tightly. "I require you with me in Portugal."

"But you really don't, Jefferson," she said, and wondered why she was bothering to repeat herself. He hadn't heard her the first time; he wouldn't hear her this time, either. He never heard anything he didn't want to hear. "The hotel can provide an assistant. Or you could take Georgia with you."

"Georgia?" His annoyance shuddered in the air around her.

Okay, fine. That was a cheap shot, she thought. No way could Georgia do the job to Jefferson's expectations. But the point is, he didn't need anyone with him.

"The work's done, Jefferson," she said, trying for calm, despite the way her stomach was jittering. "You've made the offer, the papers have been drawn up and looked over by Legal. All you have to do is sign the papers, take a tour of the ship and slap the Lyon logo on her hull. *Why* do you need me there?"

"Because," he said, his voice low and tight, "I pay you to be where I need you, when I need you. This is your job, Caitlyn."

Her head was buzzing. Her blood pumped hard and fast and her stomach did a couple of weird spins. *Her job.* And she was the first to admit it was a good one. She made a healthy salary, owned her own home—true, a condo, but still a home—and she did darn good work.

But apparently, somewhere along the way, she'd become a piece of office equipment. Steady, dependable, necessary, but as far as Jefferson was concerned, she had no more feelings than the copier that continually demanded more toner.

She hadn't expected he would take the news of her upcoming vacation lightly. But she also hadn't expected him to be such a jerk about it. Other people took vacations. Had lives. Why shouldn't *she?*

Jefferson Lyon was a man who expected everything

around him to fall into line. He walked through life issuing orders with the expectation that they would be followed. Quickly. And as much as that strength and confidence appealed to her, she was just now understanding how hard it was to live with.

Peter had been the same way, just on a smaller scale. Strong, silent, clearly in charge—and she'd gone along with him just as easily as she had with Jefferson. What in the hell did that say about *her?* Was she really so willing to lose herself in a strong man?

"You know," she mused aloud, her voice hardly more than a hush as she talked more to herself than to him, "I should have seen this coming a long time ago. But I didn't want to."

"Seen what?"

She glanced at him and noted the confusion in his eyes and the familiar stamp of irritation on his features. What was it about this man? He appealed to her on too many levels. She knew that already. And so, apparently, had Peter. But now that she thought about it, Caitlyn was forced to admit that she'd actually been drawn to Peter in the first place because he'd sort of reminded her of…*Jefferson.*

Oh, good god.

"Are you in a fugue state of some kind?" he prompted.

"Actually," she said as her emotional blinders came off and she was nearly blinded by the light, "I think I'm just coming out of one."

"Good. Then, maybe we can get some work done."

"It's the alpha-male thing," she mused, tipping her

head to one side and staring at him as if he were a smear on a glass slide under a microscope. How was it she'd never come to this realization before? How had she allowed herself to just drift in Jefferson's wake? "It has been all along. Peter. You. Even my brothers."

"What're you talking about now?"

"Revelations," she said quietly, almost amused now, as everything became clear.

"You do realize you're not making sense, right?"

"Oh, this makes perfect sense, you're just not getting it. Big surprise. And let me tell you," she said nodding for emphasis, "it took me long enough, but I've learned my lesson. I'm through with you alpha types. Give me a nice, easy-to-get-along-with beta guy. No more strong, silent, take-charge types for me. I want someone nice. Sweet. Sensitive."

His lips twisted. "Sounds more like a golden retriever."

"You would think that, of course."

"Look," Jefferson said, dipping his hands into his pants pockets, "somehow, we've gotten way off the subject. And believe it or not, I'm not really interested in your personal life. You can date whoever you want to as soon as we get back from Portugal."

"Wow. Thanks."

"Now that we have that settled," he said, dismissing her as completely as if he were swatting away an annoying gnat, "there are a few more things I need you to do before I leave for the airport. Call the pilot, tell him to be ready in an hour. Then, when you've done that, contact the Florida office. Tell them I'll be there Friday.

And cancel my appointments for the next two days. I don't know how long I'll be in Seattle and—"

She watched him as he turned for his office, plowing right ahead with the world according to Jefferson. He'd moved on and assumed she had, too. Absolutely nothing she'd said had penetrated his thick head. Her back teeth ground together, and before she could bite back the word and swallow it, she said simply, "No."

He stopped dead, turned to look at her and lifted one eyebrow. "No?"

Caitlyn took another deep breath because if she didn't she might start hyperventilating. Everything in her was demanding she sit down and wait calmly for this firestorm of emotion to fade away. So to make sure she didn't listen to that annoying, logical instinct, she moved fast. Shaking her head, she opened the bottom drawer of her desk and grabbed her purse. Slinging it over her shoulder, she snatched up her suit jacket and tossed it across her arm. "That's right. I said no."

"Caitlyn, I've taken all I'm going to take for one morning."

"And I've given all I'm going to give," she snapped. Temper spiked inside her, pushing aside all those annoying rational thoughts—and maybe that was for the best. Because, if she calmed down, took a moment to actually think about what she was doing, she'd never do it. "I'm done."

He laughed.

He actually laughed.

Then he asked, "What are you talking about?"

"I quit."

He couldn't have looked more surprised if she had announced that she was about to give birth to a Martian.

"You can't quit."

"I just did." She blinked, laid one hand on her racing heart and felt her insides slowly calm, as though someone had poured oil on a choppy sea. Strange. She waited for a jolt of panic, but it didn't come. As much as she had always loved her job, at this moment, she knew she was doing the right thing in quitting. "Wow. I actually did it. I quit."

"This is ridiculous." He took a step toward her, and she backed up just for good measure. She wasn't sure where she'd found the courage to tender her resignation, but she wasn't going to risk him talking her out of it.

Where was all of this newfound sense of spirit and independence coming from? She had no idea. Maybe it had started with Peter ending their engagement. Or maybe it had been when her fiancé had suggested that she was really in love with her boss. And maybe it was that one startling revelation that had just come to her moments ago. Whatever the reason, though, Caitlyn knew in her bones that this was the right thing to do.

She needed a fresh start. With her life. With her career. And she'd never get it if she stayed close to Jefferson Lyon. The man was too powerful. Too magnetic. Too damn sexy.

Peter was wrong about her loving Jefferson. She firmly believed that. But she wasn't foolish enough to deny the attraction she felt for the man. And how could she ever straighten out her own life when she was so near the man who could make her knees go to jelly?

"No, this makes perfect sense," she told him, rounding the edge of her desk.

"All of this over a vacation?"

"No, Jefferson," she said, feeling the swell of righteous indignation fill her. "It's about working for a man who never sees me as anything more than a convenience."

He frowned at her, his blue eyes going dark and narrow, and just for a minute, Caitlyn's courage waned. Then the phone on her desk rang and she instinctively reached for it. "Lyon Shipping."

"Caitlyn, love, it's Max again. I'd forgotten something I wanted to tell your boss."

Gritting her teeth, she said, "He's not my boss anymore, Max, but here he is."

"What? What?" Max's voice came through loud and clear as she handed the receiver to Jefferson.

"Caitlyn," Jefferson said, hanging up the phone without talking to his old friendly enemy. "I won't allow you to simply quit."

"You can't stop me, Jefferson," she said, and then left before she could stop herself from walking away from him.

A few hours later, Jefferson stormed around the perimeter of the huge room in his father's Seattle house. Outside the floor-to-ceiling windows in the old man's study, the sky was gray and spitting rain on the city as if it held a personal grudge. Trees bent in the wind coming off the Sound, and the patter of rain slashing against the windows sounded harsh in the stillness.

"If you'll sit down, we can sign these papers and finish this," his father said, following Jefferson's progress around the room. "I've got a golf game in an hour."

"Golf?" Jefferson said, stopping to wave a hand at the weather. "In this?"

Harry Lyon shrugged in his oatmeal-colored sweater. "I'm meeting friends at the club. Your mother's gone to New York for the week and—" He stopped talking, watched his son for a long moment, then said, "Why don't you tell me what's bothering you?"

"Caitlyn quit this morning."

"Your secretary?"

"Assistant."

Harry waved a hand at the distinction. "Why would she quit? She's very good at her job."

"I know," Jefferson said, shoving both hands into his pockets and turning to the window to glare at the rain.

He'd been thinking about nothing else for the last few hours. On the short flight to Seattle he'd gone over and over their argument and he still didn't understand why she'd suddenly quit. It just wasn't like her.

But then, he'd seen a whole new side to Caitlyn that morning. She'd never lost her temper with him. She'd always been the soul of professionalism. Seeing indignation and fury sparking in her eyes had caught him by surprise—something that wasn't easy to do.

"What're you going to do about it?" his father asked.

Jefferson turned his head to look at the older man.

Since retiring, his father had never looked happier. Despite—or maybe because of—the heart attack he'd experienced a few months ago, Harry Lyon was determined to enjoy his life.

Which, it turns out, is why the old man had wanted Jefferson to fly up for the day. Harry was turning over the reins to the family company. Stepping out completely. Ordinarily Jefferson would have been pleased as hell about it. He'd worked hard for this moment for years. Now, though, his mind was too full of Caitlyn's abrupt treachery to really take it all in.

"Well?" Harry prompted from his seat on an oversize leather armchair.

What was he going to do about it? There was only one answer. He was going to get her back. Jefferson Lyon didn't lose. The word wasn't even in his vocabulary. Nobody walked out on him. Not until he was damn good and ready. And he wasn't nearly ready to lose Caitlyn. The woman was too integral to his work. She knew everything. Had her pulse on the entire company.

And who would he talk to in the morning?

She was just too important to let go.

"I'll get her back," Jefferson said, his mind already sifting through scenarios, searching for just the right way to tempt her back to work. A raise? Possibly. More vacation time? He frowned. Too much of a hot button with her at the moment. A promotion to executive level? Not bad. But it was going to take more than improving her working conditions to convince Caitlyn to come back. It was going to take… A slow, sure smile curved his mouth as he realized what he was going to do about Caitlyn.

"That's what I like to hear." Harry folded his hands at his middle. "What's the plan?"

Jefferson turned his smile on his father, but he had no intention of filling the man in on this. He wouldn't approve. Wouldn't understand that the only sure way to get Caitlyn back was to seduce her into thinking it was her own idea.

If there was one thing Jefferson Lyon knew, it was women. He'd romance her, seduce her, ply her with jewelry, then act like a jerk and let her break up with him. She'd feel so bad she'd be bound to come back to work.

"Don't worry about it, Dad," he said, smiling now at the rain-washed window. "I've got it covered."

Now that she was—gulp—unemployed, Caitlyn had absolutely no reason to stick around home. Instead, she called the resort and was lucky enough to snatch up a room freed by a sudden cancellation. Another sign from the universe that she was doing the right thing. And she appreciated it.

It had felt completely liberating to stand up to Jefferson and quit her job, but now that it was done, she was having a few doubts. She'd saved plenty of her salary, so she was fine for several months moneywise, but she'd never been unemployed. Not since she'd left college. A weird sensation passed through her to know that she didn't have to be somewhere at an appointed time. Even weirder to realize she had zero obligations to worry about.

When her stomach hitched nervously as she climbed out of the cab and stood outside Fantasies, she reminded herself that she'd done the right thing. She only hoped that soon she'd believe it. Meanwhile, she'd closed up her condo and flown to the island almost a full two weeks ahead of her friends.

Janine and Debbie were completely supportive, of course, which is why they were such good friends. They'd applauded her resignation and promised to keep in touch until they were able to join her at Fantasies.

"Until then," Caitlyn whispered, getting a good grip on the handle of her suitcase as a tropical breeze kissed her skin, "you're here to relax. So get started already."

A soft island breeze danced over her skin and carried the scents of both the sea and the banks of flowers surrounding the exclusive resort. She inhaled deeply, tasting freedom and settling the jitters in her stomach at the same time.

"May I take your bag for you?"

She jolted a little and turned around to find a tall, gorgeous man in the Fantasies uniform of deep red shirt over white slacks smiling at her. "Hi."

"Hello, and welcome to Fantasies," he said, brown eyes twinkling. "Let me just take your bag inside for you."

"Thanks." She handed her suitcase off to him and followed him into the lobby, turning her head from side to side, admiring the lush flower beds on either side of the wide coral walkway. Their combined scents flavored the air with spice and the splash of a small waterfall

from somewhere nearby soothed away the last of
Caitlyn's nerves.

When she stepped into the wide-open lobby, she
came to an abrupt stop and simply stared.

Amazing was the only word for it.

The floor was cool blue tile, giving you the feeling you
were walking on water. White wicker chairs with plush
red cushions were staggered around the immense, open
lobby in clusters of conversation zones. There were several squat glass tables boasting clear crystal vases with
brilliantly colored flowers spearing out of them.

The long, serpentine registration desk wound through
the lobby in lazy curves of shining glass, behind which
were tropical fish swimming through sparkling aqua
water. Caitlyn smiled as she caught flashes of gold, red
and deep green fish darting through the sea grasses and
anemones waving in the swirling water.

Computers and telephones rested on the glass top of
the desk and the people manning their stations looked
as beautiful and perfect as the rest of this resort. Each
of them wore red shirts, white slacks and brilliant smiles
that would have made any orthodontist proud.

While she waited to register, Caitlyn accepted a crystal flute of champagne from a passing waiter and felt
the last of her doubts slip away on a contented sigh.
There would be time enough to worry about leaving
Lyon Shipping. More than time enough to worry about
finding a new job.

For right now, she was going to surrender to the lush,
indulgent vibe pulsing through this place.

* * *

Two days later, though, Caitlyn was already getting a little antsy. She was doing her best to combat the feeling. Stretched out on a red-and-white-flowered chaise, with a tall tropical drink at her side, she set her paperback down on her stomach and looked out at the water.

Miles and miles of clear, beautiful ocean stretched out in front of her and eased into shore, lapping up across powdery white sand. A cool breeze took the edge off the heat and the simple beauty of the place should have been enough to make her relax. Instead, her rotten brain kept turning back to Jefferson. The look on his face when she'd quit. The fact that now that she didn't work for him anymore, she'd probably never see him again.

But that was as it should be, right? There was nothing between them but a job she didn't have anymore. So it was better that he was out of her life.

If that were true, though, why wasn't she happier?

"I'm worried," she said into her cell phone, picking up her drink for a sip of strawberry-flavored alcohol.

"About what?" Janine demanded. "You're at the most talked-about resort on the planet. You're being waited on hand and foot. You're footloose and fancy-free. You're young and single and there must be at least a dozen men in arm's reach of you."

"True," Caitlyn admitted, letting her gaze slide across the sand and the golden-tanned bodies either laying in the sun or playing volleyball.

"So what could you possibly be worried about?"

"Jefferson," she admitted on a disgusted groan. She couldn't help it. She'd left him in the lurch, and that just didn't feel right. She'd walked out of his office and his life without any more than a moment's thought. Of course she shouldn't have quit without even giving him proper notice. For heaven's sake, she had more pride in her work than that. "I just walked out, Janine. Left him high and dry with nobody to run things."

"Just what he deserved," her friend said, then added to someone else, "Don't put baby's breath in with hydrangeas. For God's sake, were you born in a barn?"

Caitlyn smiled. The high-priced florist shop where Janine was the head designer was always busy, and Janine was always on top of everything.

"Honestly, Cait," she said on a sigh, "Lyon Shipping isn't your problem anymore. You've got to learn to let go a little. How are you supposed to have a vacation if your brain's still back here in Long Beach?"

"You're right, I know you're right," she said, taking another sip of her drink and letting the icy concoction chill the quick flash of heat she felt just at the *thought* of Jefferson Lyon. "But, Janine—"

"No buts," she interrupted. "Michael, if you break another vase, I swear, I'm going to—" The sound of breaking glass came through the phone loud and clear. "Just kill me now," Janine muttered.

Caitlyn laughed.

A minute later, though, Janine said, "Cait, get out there and meet people. *Men* people. Get drunk. Get laid. Get Jefferson Lyon out of your system."

A volleyball landed right next to her, spraying her with sand before bouncing to hit her stomach. "Hey!"

"What is it?" Janine asked.

"Attacked by a volleyball," Caitlyn muttered as the ball's owner jogged up to her, a big grin on his amazingly gorgeous face.

"Sorry about that," the guy said. "I'm Chad. Can I buy you a drink to apologize?"

"Oh, you don't have to—"

"Don't you dare turn him down," Janine ordered from a couple thousand miles away. "This is why you're there, girlfriend. To relax. To live a little."

"Umm…" Caitlyn said, listening to Janine and watching the gorgeous beach guy.

"Is he cute?"

"Uh-huh." Like-a-movie-star cute.

"Are you okay?" he asked.

"Yeah," she said. "Fine."

"Caitlyn Amanda Monroe," Janine threatened, "don't be an idiot. This is why you're there. Remember?"

She remembered. She was supposed to be relaxing. Meeting new people. Men people. And there was no time like the present to get started, she supposed.

Nodding to herself, she smiled, swallowed her nervousness and said, "Hi, Chad. I'm Caitlyn. And I'd love a drink."

Five

Caitlyn had about a half hour to shower and dress before meeting Chad for drinks in the main bar. She hurried down the long, tiled hallway to her own door, digging in her pocket for the key card as she ran. She shouldn't have agreed to meet the guy for a drink. And if Janine hadn't been on the phone with her at the time, she wouldn't have.

She just wasn't feeling very sociable at the moment. Not that she wasn't interested in meeting new people—men people—it was just that she was too busy thinking about Jefferson to appreciate someone else. Even someone as gorgeous as Chad.

"Which is just sick and twisted and wrong," she muttered, dropping her tote bag on the end of the bed. "Why you should be thinking about your *former* boss at all is a mystery. He's gone. Out of your life. Kaput. *Adios, amigo. Sayonara. Ciao. Arrivederci.*"

"That's two in Italian."

"Yikes!" Caitlyn clutched at her throat, spun around on her heel, lost her balance and tumbled back across the bed. Eyes wide, heart racing, she stared at Jefferson as he walked casually out of her bathroom. A thick fog of misting steam rolled out the open door behind him, surrounding him in a haze that made him look almost otherworldly. Of course, the towel hooked around the waist of his naked body wasn't helping the situation any.

His hair was wet and drops of water were still rolling across his tanned, much-more-muscled-than-she'd-dreamed chest. And his piercing blue eyes were locked on hers. His full, delicious-looking mouth quirked in a half smile as she pushed herself up to a sitting position.

"Surprise."

"*Surprise?* What do you mean, *surprise?* What are you doing here?" She held up a hand as her heartbeat slowed from frantic down to way too fast. "Scratch that. Never mind what you're doing here. What are you doing *here?* In my room here, I mean. How did you get in? Why would you— How could you—" She broke off, gulped some air and then settled for glaring at him.

Jefferson shrugged, and Caitlyn couldn't help but watch the play of muscles that shifted with that minor action. But she steadfastly kept her gaze *above* that towel. Oh, boy, she could be in some serious trouble here. No, she wasn't in love with her boss, but she was clearly quite deeply in lust with him.

And seeing him in that towel and a few drops of water was enough to make any woman start drooling.

"I came to bring you back home," he said. "Back to Long Beach. Back to the company."

Of course that's why he was here. God, she was such an idiot. Taking a shower in her room only meant that he had needed a shower and helped himself. It *didn't* mean that he was here for *her*. Naturally, the only thing on Jefferson's mind was the usual. Himself.

"I quit, remember?"

He laughed, and the sound echoed off the walls of her large, elegant room. "You can't quit, Caitlyn. Work is your life. How do you quit your life?"

"That was then. This is now. I'm making a new life, thanks."

"One without me. Without Lyon Shipping."

"That's the plan." The fact that she'd actually missed him in the last two days didn't speak of great success for that plan, but that was neither here nor there.

"Hmm…I wonder."

"Come on, Jefferson," she said, wanting to get him off the subject of her entirely. "You didn't come all the way here just to convince me to come back to a job I quit. Why are you really here?"

"After you left," he said, walking across the room toward her, his footsteps silent on the thick, pale blue carpet, "I realized something."

She scooted back on the bed, keeping her distance, but then thought about being on the bed with him so close and so conveniently naked. Which made her shoot off the mattress as though there was a spring under her behind. "What? You realized what?"

"I needed a vacation."

"Right," she said, shaking her head at the ridiculous story. "You've *never* taken a vacation, Jefferson. The closest you came to it was when you were flying around the globe ruining *my* vacations. Besides, shouldn't you be back at the office, annoying some minion into finalizing your Portugal trip?"

"You're exactly right. I have never taken a vacation, so I was more than due. As to ruining your vacations in the past, I'm not here to do that again. I'm only here to join in the fun."

"Fun?"

"As to the Portugal trip," he said, swiping one hand through his wet hair, "my rather exceptional admin has everything taken care of already."

Exceptional.

He'd called her *exceptional*. Oh, he was up to something.

She only wished she knew what.

"And," he admitted with another shrug—and he really did have some amazing pecs— "I missed you."

Caitlyn snorted. Very inelegant, she knew, but she just couldn't help herself. Oh, yes. Definitely up to something. "You missed me. Sure you did. You mean, you missed having me run interference between you and the company. It's only been a couple of days, Jefferson."

A couple of days during which she had missed him. But that wasn't the point now, was it?

"This isn't about work, Caitlyn," he said, his gaze fixed on her so steadily she was pretty sure she could feel heat sizzling in the air between them. "This is about *us*."

She just stared at him for a long minute. This was getting weirder and weirder. First, he's naked in her hotel room. Next he's missing her. Now he's talking about an *us*?

"Okay, I must have somehow slipped into an alternate dimension," she muttered, shaking her head and fiddling with the cloth belt of her cover-up. No way was she slipping it off to stand in front of him in her bathing suit. The more clothes she had on at the moment, the safer she'd be.

And *where* was all this sudden, desperate lust coming from? She'd worked for the man for three long years. Sure, she'd been attracted, but she'd never felt the kind of swamping, all-encompassing heat that was boiling in her system at the moment. Was it the fact that they were both away from the business setting?

Or maybe it was just that towel he was wearing.

Her eyes popped a little. Was that towel *slipping?*

"Alternate dimension," she repeated numbly. She blinked, tore her gaze from the towel. "That has to be it. The only rational explanation. Well, that or I'm having a stroke. No, not a stroke. Must be the alternate-plane thing. The elevator. I probably got caught in one of those ripples in time. Maybe if I go back down, I'll get back to my own universe and none of this will be happening."

"Ripple in time?"

Her gaze snapped to his. "Makes more sense than believing any of this is happening."

"But it is happening," he said in a voice that had dropped low enough that the vibrations of it were sizzling along every one of her nerve endings.

"No, it's not," she said firmly. No way was she going to get sucked into whatever game he was playing. She wasn't going to go back to work for him. She was sticking to her guns—and not going to look at that towel.

"Jefferson," she said, inching farther from him. "Let's forget for the moment why you came here. How did you get into my room?"

He smiled and she felt her knees wobble. Not a good sign.

"I followed you here."

"Yeah. I got that." Frowning, she asked, "How'd you know where I was going?"

"It's not that difficult for a man in my position to get whatever answers he needs, Caitlyn."

Probably not, she mused. The man had contacts all over the world and enough money to pay for whatever information he needed. But why go to all this trouble? And even if finding her was no big deal, how the hell did he get into her hotel room?

"Fine. You found me. But who let you into my room?"

He sat down on the edge of the bed and the towel pulled away from one of his thighs, exposing a good bit of tanned, very muscular flesh with just a sprinkling of blond hair. *Oh, god.*

"When I explained to the front desk that my wife had arrived a few days ahead of me, they were very happy to give me a key."

"Your *wife?*" Okay, that was enough to pull her out of the fantasies her brain was currently indulging in. "You told them I was your wife? And they believed you?"

"Of course."

Of course.

He said it as a matter of fact. And why wouldn't he? The name Jefferson Lyon carried enough weight that they probably would have let him into her room even if he *hadn't* claimed to be her husband. Money, as she'd learned long ago, didn't just talk, it *shouted.*

"Caitlyn," he was saying, and she forced her over-worked mind to focus. "There were no other rooms available. The hotel was completely booked up. So what else was I supposed to do?"

"Go home?" she offered, throwing both hands high in exasperation.

"Not without seeing you." He casually leaned back and propped himself up on his elbows. The towel slipped again and Caitlyn sucked in air. Now most of his thick thigh was exposed, with the soft blue towel just covering up the essentials.

Closing her eyes, Caitlyn rubbed at the spot between her eyes and told herself to count to ten. When she'd finished, she counted to twenty. Didn't help. She was still furious and a little shocked and a *lot* needy.

So not a good combo.

Jefferson watched her and wished he could read her mind. The emotions flitting across her features were fleeting and so diverse he knew that her thoughts had to be wildly entertaining.

While she began to pace, talking to herself, Jefferson followed her with his gaze. Sunlight speared through the open French doors leading to the small private balcony. A soft wind made the sheer curtains dance and wave with languid abandon and the wash of golden light in the room played on Caitlyn's long, lean legs, tanned to the color of warm honey. Something stirred within him and he scowled briefly as he recalled the desk clerk describing Caitlyn as "the one with the amazing legs."

Jefferson had to admit the guy had been right. And why had he never noticed Caitlyn's legs before? Shaking his head now, he pushed that stray thought out of his mind and concentrated instead on the situation. He was here with her and his plan was just getting started.

He could have gone downstairs to find her, but meeting her this way had been so much more…intriguing. He hadn't had any trouble talking his way into Caitlyn's room—and if he owned this particular resort, he'd have fired the clerk who'd bowed to Jefferson's name and money long enough to hand over the key to a guest's room. But since that employee wasn't his trouble, he could only appreciate the fact that the Lyon name carried the weight he had needed.

Of course, the fact that Jefferson had bought up the remaining rooms in the hotel so he wouldn't be able to leave Caitlyn's room had probably convinced the desk jockey to be more lenient than usual.

"You can't stay here," she said finally.

"No choice. There aren't any available rooms."

"Go buy a house."

"Private island," he reminded her.

Hands at her hips, she lifted her chin and glared at him. "Not my problem."

"Now, is that any way for a wife to talk to her husband?"

"I can't believe you did that. In fact, I'm surprised you managed to choke out the word *wife*."

Jefferson pushed off the bed, felt the towel at his hips slip a little and reached to straighten it. And he caught the flash of interest in Caitlyn's eyes. Smiling, he said, "But I did. And now that I have, you're stuck with me."

"Don't count on it," she promised, and walked to the phone on the nightstand beside the bed. "I'll call the front desk. Tell them you lied."

He folded his arms over his chest. "I'll tell them this is a lover's quarrel."

"They won't believe you."

"I can be *very* convincing."

She frowned up at him and he wanted to grin at the frustration pouring off her in waves. He could almost see her thinking her way through this mess and looking for a way out. When she didn't find one, she said, "Fine.

Fine, they'd side with you anyway and probably end up kicking *me* out and giving you *my* room."

"Oh," Jefferson said, enjoying himself, "that wouldn't happen. I'd never let my 'wife' be treated like that."

She blew out a breath that ruffled the fringe of bangs on her forehead. "You're such a jerk."

"Pet names," he said, smiling. "Isn't that nice?"

"I don't know what you're up to, Jefferson," she said. "But it won't work, whatever it is."

"What's the matter? Afraid to be alone with me?"

"That's ridiculous."

"Is it?" One eyebrow rose. "Then, there's no problem, is there?"

"Fine. You can stay here until they find a room for you."

Which wouldn't happen anytime soon, Jefferson knew all too well.

"But you sleep on the floor."

"So you are scared of me. Or of yourself *with* me."

"Your ego is astounding."

"Thank you."

"I can't believe this is happening," she muttered.

"Now, Caitlyn," he said, striding toward the closet where the few clothes he'd grabbed before this hurried trip were already hung alongside hers. "We don't want to start our vacation with an argument, do we?"

"What're you doing?"

He glanced at her over his shoulder. "Getting dressed."

"Here?"

"Where else?" He dropped both hands to the towel

and unhooked it. Before he could let it fall, she was sprinting for the bathroom.

"Just…get dressed and go away. I have to get ready for a date."

"A *date?*"

She paused in the bathroom doorway and tossed him a satisfied smile. "Yes, a date. Just enjoying 'our' vacation, Jefferson."

She closed the door and he dropped the towel in disgust. She'd been there two days and already had a date? Didn't bode well for his seduction plans. But then he reassured himself that by getting her to let him stay in her room, he'd already won the first round. She just didn't know it.

Besides, he thought as he grabbed his clothes and got dressed, just because she *had* a date didn't mean that she was going to stay on it for long.

Caitlyn smiled at Chad as he regaled her with yet another tale of his prowess at day-trading. She was almost asleep with her eyes open when he asked, "Can you believe it? I traded that stock with an eighth of a percent profit. Tightest deal I'd ever swung." He sighed and leaned back in his chair, clearly enjoying the memory of his triumph. "Nothing more vicious than the market."

"Sounds fascinating." She picked up her drink and wished it were full. Would it be rude to signal the waiter for a refill? She didn't think she could take much more of this without slipping into a coma.

Her mother's words of warning about handsome men

came rushing back to her. *Sometimes, honey, God gives and God takes away. Lots of times, handsome faces cover up empty heads.*

God, she hated when her mother was right.

"Hello."

Caitlyn jumped in her chair, whipped a quick look over her shoulder and couldn't believe how happy she was to see Jefferson standing right behind her. Of course, she couldn't let *him* know that. She wanted him to believe she was having a good time. Without him.

"Hello," Chad said, shooting a confused look from her to Jefferson and back again.

Jefferson leaned down, planted a quick kiss on Caitlyn's cheek. And before her skin had stopped buzzing with heat, he was smiling at Chad and extending his hand. "Caitlyn, darling," he said affably, "you didn't tell me someone else would be joining us for drinks. I'm sorry I got hung up on the phone. But you know how those business calls can run on."

"Umm…" She watched him take a seat beside her, signal the waiter with a quick wave of his hand and then drop his arm around her shoulders. Caitlyn tried to shift out from under his grasp, but he only tightened his hold on her.

The man sitting across from them looked more confused than ever, and Caitlyn couldn't blame him.

"So, sweetie," Jefferson said, "who's your friend?"

"The name's Chad."

"Really? *Chad?*"

"Jefferson…" Caitlyn muttered.

"Look," Chad said tightly as the waiter appeared, took Jefferson's order and quietly disappeared again, "I don't know what's going on here, but Caitlyn and I had a date for drinks and—"

"A date?" Jefferson laughed, and his amusement seemed to hit Chad the wrong way. Again, Caitlyn couldn't really blame him. She wasn't amused, either. Though, damned if she wasn't relieved that Jefferson had shown up.

What was the old saying? Better the devil you know?

"What's so funny?" Chad demanded, getting a little red in the face.

"Nothing." Jefferson's smile faded and his eyes narrowed to dangerous blue slits. "I always find the fact that a man thinks he has a date with my wife entertaining."

"Your *wife?*" Chad stood up and shot Caitlyn a quelling look.

"Jefferson—Chad—"

"You're not wearing a ring." The darkly attractive, extremely boring man looked at Jefferson. "She didn't say anything about a husband, man."

"Well, we did have an argument earlier. She's probably still upset with me. Isn't that right, darling?" He pulled her in for a quick kiss, and while her lips burned with a fire that seemed to keep right on sizzling, Caitlyn's voice dried up.

"I didn't mean to come on to her—"

"I understand." Benevolent now, Jefferson nodded and flicked his fingers at the man looking for a quick escape. "My wife is a beautiful woman. Hardly surprising you'd try to make a move. Now, though, if you'll excuse us…"

Chad disappeared so fast Caitlyn half expected to see sparks shooting up from the heels of his shoes. Then she was alone with Jefferson. "Why are you doing this?"

He gave her shoulders another squeeze and smiled down at her. "Rescuing you from boredom, you mean? Well, because I'm a great humanitarian."

"How do you know I was bored?" she countered. "Chad was fascinating. Seriously. I was hanging on his every word."

"Your eyes were glazed over and your body language indicated imminent unconsciousness."

Caitlyn sighed, slipped out from under Jefferson's arm and picked up her drink. Draining it, she held the empty glass up to him, and once again he signaled for the waiter. What was the point in pretending? She was too grateful that Jefferson had arrived like the cavalry. If he hadn't, she might have been stuck for hours listening to tales of pork bellies and futures trading. "Fine. I admit it. I've never been so bored in my life."

"What did you expect?" he asked, grinning. "The man's name is *Chad*. Is that even a name? Isn't it really just a hanging piece of paper?"

Caitlyn chuckled. "Stop it. He seemed nice enough on the beach."

"Aah, well. You met on the beach. Of course you'd expect him to be fascinating. Probably heatstroke."

"He's handsome."

"So am I."

She shook her head at him. "Don't forget humble."

"Goes without saying." He sat up, leaned his elbows on the glass table and looked into her eyes.

All around them, the small, round glass tables were full as the resort's guests gathered to watch the sunset from the comfort of an elegant bar. Beyond the sweep of the sparkling glass walls separating the bar from the patio outside, the sun sank toward the sea in a glorious blend of vibrant colors that washed the surface of the ocean with reflected glory.

Crystal clinked. The whispered hush of conversation rose and fell all around them. And music, something slow and bluesy, piped in from discreetly hidden speakers.

Jefferson's blue eyes were locked on her and Caitlyn felt the power of them sink deep inside. If she didn't *know* that he was up to something… Never mind—she *did* know and that was all that mattered.

She tried to ignore the romantic atmosphere and the fact that her mouth was still sort of humming from the casual, too-quick kiss he'd given her for Chad's benefit. So, despite the fact that she really wished he were serious, that she really wished he *did* want her, Caitlyn steeled herself against her own desires.

"Jefferson," she said as the waiter delivered her fresh raspberry martini, "tell me what's really going on."

He leaned in closer, keeping his gaze locked with hers and heat poured through her in a thick ripple. "Why is it so hard for you to believe that I'm here because I missed you? Because I realized that you were…more than just my admin. That you were important."

Caitlyn blew out a long breath, lifted her drink and took a sip of the icy liquid. It didn't affect the roaring heat within her, but it did help ease the knot in her throat. "We worked together for three years, Jefferson. If I'm so important, why did it take you so long to notice?"

He gave her a smile that was wicked. "Because it wasn't until you'd gone that it hit me." He reached across the table, took her hand and smoothed the pad of his thumb across her skin in slow strokes. "You're… important to me, Caitlyn."

Her stomach jumped and her heart jolted hard against her ribs. Oh, if she thought for even a moment that he was telling the truth, she'd leap across the table and kiss him as she used to dream about doing. But how could she believe that? How could she trust that a man who changed women with as much ease as he changed shirts could suddenly want only her?

She pulled her hand free and shook her head. "No, Jefferson. Whatever it is you're up to, I'm not going to fall for it."

"Right now," he said, standing up, then drawing her to her feet, "what I'm up to is a sunset stroll on the beach. Would you like to join me? Or do I make you too nervous?"

Six

She didn't go on the moonlight stroll with him.

She didn't feel sorry for him as he complained in a barely concealed mutter while he tried to fall asleep on the too-short couch of her suite.

She didn't feel guilty as she stretched luxuriously in her wide, empty king-size bed the last few nights. Especially if she wished—maybe—for company in that bed.

Caitlyn knew Jefferson all too well. He was up to something, whether he was forced to admit it or not. He wasn't a man to come crawling after a recalcitrant employee. He wasn't the type to crowd his way into her life without a self-serving reason.

And whatever he had planned, Caitlyn had no intention of making it easy on him. She was through with Lyon Shipping *and* Jefferson Lyon.

Now, if only he would go away.

Because nothing short of that was going to keep her sane. Three days of his constant presence, his persistent…attention, and Caitlyn was weakening. She felt it. The man had more charm, more personal power than anyone she'd ever known. And when he chose to focus that power on one woman, he was nearly irresistible.

When she went for a swim, he was there. When she stopped in the bar for a drink, he was there. When she took a surfing lesson and spent more time facedown in the ocean than standing on the board, he was there.

Which was exactly why she'd left the resort that morning for a walk into the small village the owner of Fantasies had had built for his employees. The only people on the privately owned island were the hotel guests and the resort staff, who lived in postcard-perfect cottages sprinkled across the island. The village contained both necessity stores and opulent gift shops where tourists were tempted to spend whatever money they had left after paying their hotel bill.

The only vehicles allowed on the island were electric golf carts and bicycles, so the main street made of brick was mostly empty and almost pristinely clean. The sidewalks were neatly swept and lined with flower boxes, spilling brilliant color and heavy scent into the sun-warmed air. Shop windows gleamed and displayed everything from fashionable clothing to designer jewelry.

Tourists wandered, cameras firmly fixed to their eyes and shoppers loaded down with brightly colored gift bags made their way back up the hill to the resort.

Caitlyn ignored all of it. "He's making me crazy," she admitted into her cell phone.

Janine sighed heavily. "He's got a plan."

"Well, yeah. I just don't know what it is."

"I wish I was there, but— Damn it, Michael, the ferns go in the box *first,* not on top of the roses—I just can't get away from here early."

"I know." Caitlyn sighed, too. If Janine and Debbie were here, she'd be able to keep herself busy with her friends. She'd be able to avoid Jefferson much more easily than she could now. Of course, she'd still have to deal with him being in her room every night, but at least she'd have the daytime hours to keep him out of her mind.

"He's still staying in your room, isn't he?" Janine demanded.

"I checked with the front desk just this morning. They claim to be full up, so there's nowhere for him to go."

"You could still toss his butt out and make him sleep by the pool or something."

A good thought, she admitted, then shook her head and stepped around a cranky toddler being dragged along the street by his mother. But she knew she'd never do it. "No," she said. "I can't do that."

"So…what?" Janine asked. "Instead, you'll let him ruin your vacation? You don't owe him anything, Cait. You quit, remember?"

"Of course I remember, but—"

"No buts," Janine cut her off neatly. "He's working you for a reason, Cait— Michael, for the love of God, go up and wait on customers. If you keep trying to arrange those flowers I'm gonna beat you to death with 'em." She blew out a breath, then said, "I swear, if I don't get to that island soon, this shop is going to be a bloodbath."

Caitlyn laughed and it felt good. "You talk a good game, Janine, but we both know you're just not the violent type."

"I could learn."

"Caitlyn!" A deep voice called her name and she stopped dead on the sidewalk.

"Oh, god," she whispered into her phone as she turned around to watch Jefferson striding toward her. "He found me. Damn it, he tracked me into town and he found me."

"It's a small island," Janine reminded her. "How hard could it be?"

"Oh, he looks so good," Caitlyn said. He'd come to the island in such a hurry he hadn't packed many clothes. Instead, he'd bought a new wardrobe here in the village. And these clothes were nothing like what she was used to seeing him in.

Normally, he was a three-piece-suit kind of man. Elegantly cut. Perfectly tailored. The ultimate alpha male in charge of his world. But here on the island he was wearing casual clothing that managed to make him look amazing and all too…approachable. Today, he was wearing summer-white slacks and a short-sleeved dark red shirt, open at the collar to display a vee of tanned skin that had Caitlyn's fingertips itching to touch it.

His tawny hair looked a little lighter from all the sun and his eyes looked even bluer than usual. He was clutching a cell phone to his ear, though, and the frown on his face didn't bode well for whoever he was talking to.

"Earth to Caitlyn!"

"Huh?" Janine's voice shrieked in her ear, but all Caitlyn heard was an annoying buzzing of sound. How could she think about anything but Jefferson when he was walking toward her, spearing his gaze into hers?

"Caitlyn, get a grip. Don't let him get to you. You've got to be strong. You've got to—"

"I'll call you back," Caitlyn said, and folded up her phone in the middle of Janine's tirade.

Jefferson stopped in front of her, held up one hand to keep her from speaking and said with an exaggerated patience, "The Peterson contracts are in the file, Georgia." He rolled his eyes, blew out an impatient breath and demanded, "Look again."

Caitlyn winced in sympathy. Poor Georgia. The older woman was as nervous as a fire walker when she had to speak directly to Jefferson. No doubt, Georgia's nerves were making her even more helpless than usual.

"No," Jefferson said, and gave Caitlyn a glare that plainly said, *This is all your fault for quitting.* "I don't care if you've already looked and can't find them. Look again. The contracts were to be sent to Legal this morning. If you can't find—"

"Oh, for heaven's sake, give me the phone." Caitlyn wiggled her fingers for it, and when he handed it to her, she said, "Georgia, hi. This is Caitlyn."

Instantly, the other woman started babbling about broken copiers, a secretary who was out sick and the three letters she still had to get out before the end of the day. Panic trilled across the phone lines and had Caitlyn sighing.

"Relax, okay? Everything will get done." She looked at Jefferson, who was watching her with barely concealed fury. Forgetting about him, she focused on the woman hyperventilating on the phone. "First thing, though, you need to get the contracts down to Legal. The Peterson contracts are in the file, I put them there myself. It's okay. Go look again and take your time. I'll wait."

"The woman is incompetent," Jefferson muttered, and shoved both hands into the pockets of his slacks. Irritation stamped on his features, he looked like a king who needed to lop off someone's head.

"No, she's not. You make her nervous."

"She makes *me* crazy," he countered irritably.

"That's because you're so impati— Georgia!" Smiling, Caitlyn nodded at Jefferson. "Good. You found them. No, don't worry. Just take them down to Legal yourself. There's still plenty of time. You're welcome," she said. "And it was good talking to you, too."

Closing the phone, she tossed it back to Jefferson with a shake of her head. "Crisis averted."

He tucked his phone into the breast pocket of his shirt. "Only because you took care of it."

"You could have done it, too," she said, turning away and continuing on her walk up the narrow street. Pausing now and then to look in a shop window, she slanted him a glance. "You just don't know how to talk to people."

"Excuse me?"

She faced him, tilting her head back to look him directly in the eye. "You give orders, Jefferson. You don't talk."

"I'm the boss."

"And trust me when I say everyone knows it."

"Everyone but you."

"You're not my boss, anymore," she pointed out, and ignored the tiny, tiny, tiny twinge of regret that pinged inside her. Then she started walking again, determined to enjoy the sun on her face and the cool ocean wind that rushed through the tidy village.

"I should be," he muttered, and shortened his long stride to keep pace beside her. "You shouldn't have quit, Caitlyn. That phone call only defines the fact that you have your finger on the pulse of my company."

She had to admit it was good to hear him say so. Everyone wanted to know that their efforts were appreciated. That their work was noticed. Too bad she'd had to quit to get him to realize it.

"You belong with me, Caitlyn."

"What?" She stopped dead outside a jewelry store and looked up at him.

He scowled at her. "You heard me. You belong with me. With Lyon Shipping."

"Aah…" *Idiot,* she told herself, turning her gaze from him to the shop window. Of course he'd been talking about her job. He hadn't meant that he'd wanted her for *himself.* That's what all of this was about, she knew it. Whether he was willing to admit it or not, he was here, on this island, tempting her, because he missed his trusty assistant.

Here she'd been torn over the lusty, needy feelings ripping through her like lightning strikes, and he was simply trying to woo her back to work. Well, she was done. He could do his damnedest, but she wasn't going back to her old life. This was the new and improved Caitlyn. She wasn't going to bury her own wants and needs anymore for the sake of everyone else.

Jefferson watched her expression change from surly to needy in a blink. And he smiled to himself, suddenly feeling on surer ground. Talking to Georgia had had him ready to tear out his own hair. Then watching Caitlyn disarm the situation with almost no effort at all had only served to feed his own conviction that he needed to get her back and he wasn't making any headway.

Now, though, he had another idea. "What are you staring at?"

"Those," she said, and tapped a fingernail against the glass. Gold earrings dazzling with drops of emerald and topaz shone in the sun, and Jefferson knew exactly what to do. What he should have done from the moment he'd arrived on this blasted island.

He wanted to seduce her, not annoy her. He should have been pulling the big guns out from the beginning. But it wasn't too late to start.

"Come on." He grabbed her upper arm despite her token protests, opened the door and pulled her into the shop.

A few minutes later they were out on the street again, leaving a delighted shopkeeper toting up his profits. The earrings hung from Caitlyn's ears and winked at him when she turned her head.

"You shouldn't have bought them," she said, reaching up to touch them, stroking the cold, beautiful stones as if they were alive and needed petting. "And I shouldn't have taken them," she added.

"Why not?"

She blew out a breath and turned her face into the wind. Her hair lifted away and the earrings caught the sunlight, dazzling against her skin. "Because. They're too expensive."

"If you're insisting on quitting, consider them severance pay."

"I already got my—"

Irritation flamed. "Caitlyn, for God's sake, it's a pair of earrings. They look good on you. Enjoy them."

She smiled and shook her head just to feel the earrings dance against her neck. "Okay, then. Thank you."

A tight knot inside him eased as she accepted the earrings, and he didn't look too closely at the reason behind his pleasure. After all, what mattered was that he continue seducing her into trusting him so that he could get her back to work. Where she belonged.

The earrings looked better on Caitlyn than they had in the display case. And as much as he knew jewelry, he knew women better. The earrings had been just the right touch. All women responded to gifts. And spontaneous gifts most of all. She was softening toward him, even if she didn't want to.

And judging that the time was right for another move, he made it before she could close up on him again.

"You can thank me by having dinner with me tonight."

Her surprisingly luscious mouth curved in a reluctant smile. "You mean, on purpose? Not just because you happen to show up and chase off whoever else might be at my table?"

"Do your admirers a favor," he said, bristling slightly at the memory of just how many of the men at this resort kept homing in on Caitlyn. Despite the fact that he'd introduced himself as her husband. "Give them a night off."

"Why should I?"

He shrugged as if it didn't matter to him in the slightest. "The question is, why not? You're not afraid to be alone with me, are you?"

She should have been afraid. She could feel her insides softening toward Jefferson, and Caitlyn knew she was on dangerous ground. The moment she stepped out onto the moonlit patio to find that he had arranged for them to have a "private" dinner, she realized that the ground was even more dangerous than she had suspected.

It was a beautiful setting. The full moon shone down from an inky black sky speckled with stars. The ocean's dark surface reflected the light in hazy patterns and a soft breeze made the flames on the twin taper candles dance and sway.

Jefferson was standing beside the table, wearing the suit and tie he'd arrived in. His hair was neatly swept back from his forehead and he looked the very image of a rich, powerful playboy. When he smiled at her Caitlyn felt her knees go to water and she deliberately locked them into place to keep from falling onto her face.

The heels of her sandals clicked against the flag-stone patio as she walked to join him. She shivered slightly when the breeze slid across her shoulders, bare in the strapless deep-green-colored dress she'd pur-chased in the village. Her new earrings hung at her ears and brushed against her neck with every step.

He'd bought her jewelry. Just as he had all the other women in his life. The ones he'd been trying to seduce and the ones he'd been trying to get rid of. She'd seen first-hand how Jefferson used charm and gifts to sway wom-en into his way of thinking. And she was determined to keep from becoming just one of the masses at his feet.

Steeling herself with that thought, she stopped beside him and accepted the glass of chilled white wine he handed her. "This is beautiful."

"Yes," he said, his gaze moving over her in a slow, deliberate sweep. "You are."

A hum of something electrified stirred within her and Caitlyn had to fight to remember why she wasn't going to be seduced by a man who had way too many exes already. "It's not going to work, you know?"

"What's that?" He leaned back against the scrolled iron railing and smiled at her.

"Seducing me," she said, and took a sip of wine to ease her dry throat. Then she took another sip to try to still the frantic race of her heart.

"Is that what I'm doing?"

She hoped so.

No, she didn't.

Oh, hell. Yes, she did.

"It's what you always do," she said, carrying her wine with her as she walked a few steps away from him. Staring out at the ocean, she felt the kiss of the wind, inhaled the scent of the sea and used them both to steady herself. "You're a generous man, Jefferson, but you buy jewelry for women for two reasons only." She turned her head to look at him and saw the bemused expression on his face.

"Is that right?"

"Yep." She braced her arms on the cold iron railing, and still watching him, said, "You're either trying to seduce me or get rid of me. And since we both know it's not the latter…that really only leaves one option."

He walked closer and she caught the tangy, spicy scent of his aftershave. She'd been surrounded by that scent for days now, sharing her hotel room with him, fighting for bathroom space and always, always having his scent all around her.

"You know me so well, Caitlyn," he said softly, taking a spot beside her on the rail. His arm brushed against hers, and even through the fabric of his suit coat, Caitlyn felt heat pour into her body from that small point of contact.

"Better, I think, than you know," she said.

He reached out, brushed a strand of her hair back and tucked it behind her ear, trailing the tips of his fingers over her skin. She shivered.

"Well, then," he said, "if I'm trying to seduce you... how am I doing?"

"Not bad," she admitted, though it cost her, since there was an invisible fist tightening around her throat, making breathing, much less talking, difficult.

"Let's see if I can't improve on things then," he whispered, and took her wineglass from suddenly nerveless fingers. Setting it down on the table behind him, he turned her in his arms, stared down at her for the longest moment of Caitlyn's life and then slowly lowered his head to hers.

She should stop him.

She knew that she should back away now and run screaming into the night. Kissing Jefferson would only make an unbearable situation that much more difficult.

But she wasn't going anywhere, so she told herself she might as well stop pretending otherwise.

His mouth touched hers. Once. Twice. Soft, quick kisses that jump-started her heart and had her stomach doing dips and spins in heady anticipation. That slight brush of his lips to hers made her feel heat that she'd never known before. Made her want him as she'd never wanted anything in her life. Made her hungry for the taste of him.

And just when she hoped he would kiss her more thoroughly, more completely, he pulled his head back and she opened her eyes to look up at him. He was frowning and his eyes glittered with an emotion she couldn't read.

As she stood in his grasp, every nerve ending bristling, he looked at her as if he'd never seen her before and ran the tips of his fingers along her cheek. "Sweet," he whispered. "So soft and sweet."

His gaze moved over her, studying her as if trying to puzzle something out. But then the moment passed and fire leaped into his eyes. His hands slid up and down her bare arms and his touch was like a flame.

"Jefferson..."

"Another taste," he said so quietly his voice was almost lost in the rush of the sea below them. "I have to have another taste."

Hunger erupted between them, and this time, when he bent his head to hers, he took more than a simple brush of mouth to mouth. This time he plundered her. Hard, ferocious, his mouth took hers in a frenzy of need that she felt echoing within. He parted her lips with his tongue, and Caitlyn sighed into him as she felt the damp heat invade her.

Her legs wobbled, and deep inside her, she felt liquid warmth pool at her center and ache for what only he could give her. His strong hands moved up and down her spine, then slipped to her behind and held her pressed tightly to the hard, rigid length of him.

Caitlyn lost herself in the magic of the moment. She

forgot all about her determination to avoid Jefferson's seductive powers. Forgot all about the fact that she knew he was deliberately toying with her. Didn't care that his amazing kiss meant no more to him than it had with any of the other women in his life.

For now, for right now, this was enough.

She was pliant in his arms. Warm and curvy and eager. Jefferson knew that in a seduction, timing was everything. He should slow down now. Back away before he pushed her too far too quickly. Seduction was a slow, deliberate business. A careful dance to which he knew all the steps.

And yet, he didn't want to stop kissing her. She melded against him, and his body went tighter, harder than he would have thought possible. Every inch of him ached for her. His hands held her to him, ground her hips against his, and it wasn't enough.

He took her mouth, invaded her damp heat, and it wasn't enough. Felt her breath puff against his cheek and only wanted more. Heard her soft sigh and felt himself inflamed at the gentle sound. Her scent welled up inside him, flowers and spice, and flavored her kiss until he thought he would never again draw a breath without tasting her.

And that thought was enough to drag him back to his senses—or what was left of them. Reluctantly, he tore his mouth from hers and eased her from the iron grip he'd held her in. He had to let her go if for no other reason than to prove to himself that he could.

But when she turned those big, dark eyes on him, Jefferson knew that whether or not he was touching her, the connection was still there. Linking them together. Drawing them closer.

He took a step back to give himself time to settle, turned and picked up their wineglasses. Handing her one, he took a long drink of the chilled wine and let the icy liquid cool the fires burning within.

"Okay," she said, and swallowed hard. "That was better than not bad."

"Yeah," he agreed, taking her hand and leading her to her chair, "it was."

Much better. The seduction was working just as he'd planned. But if he wasn't careful, he might just get caught in his own web.

Seven

A couple of days later Caitlyn felt as though she were balanced on a delicately thin wire stretched taut, high over a cage filed with hungry lions.

"Or," she told herself, "make that one very hungry *Lyon*."

Who would have guessed that Jefferson could pack so much power into a kiss? That she could feel all she'd felt in those few moments on that moonlit patio? Want all she'd wanted. And in the past two days he'd been even more attentive. Going with her for swims, into the village to shop, having dinner with her, glaring at any men who might think about approaching.

The man was a force of nature. Irresistible, overwhelming and just so damned appealing.

Oh, she was in serious trouble.

She leaned back in her chair and let her gaze wander over the elegant yet sleekly casual resort restaurant. The floor here was blue tile, as well, and the walls were a soft sea-green. One side of the room was glass with French doors leading onto a patio with the ocean just beyond. There weren't many customers at the moment, as it was too late for lunch and too early for dinner. Caitlyn had come in and ordered tea and scones. She'd simply needed a quiet place to sit and think. Somewhere away from her former boss and current pain in the behind.

And it had been quiet. Until her cell phone rang a moment ago.

"Oh," Debbie said firmly, "he's hungry, all right. Just make sure he doesn't start snacking on you."

Caitlyn frowned. Her friend had a point. Although, the thought of being nibbled by Jefferson did have its appeal.

"Oh, man," she said on a groan, "this is bad."

"That's why I called. Janine told me you're having some problems with Jefferson," Debbie said, and Caitlyn calmed down just listening to her more even-tempered friend's quiet voice coming over the phone.

"Problems. Oh, that's fair to say," she said, picking at the corner of one blueberry scone. "He's throwing me off balance because he's being so *nice.*"

"Uh-huh."

She heard the disbelief in her friend's tone and couldn't really blame her. After all, Debbie and Janine had been her listening posts to all of her complaints about Jefferson for the last three years. But they didn't understand, really. As much as she'd always grumbled about him, Caitlyn had enjoyed working for him more than she'd disliked it.

"Okay, fine, he wasn't always an easy man to get along with, but here he's different."

"I bet."

"In a good way," Caitlyn said, feeling for some strange reason that she should be defending him even though he'd been making her nuts. "He's funny, too, Debbie. God, at dinner the other night we laughed for hours. I'd never really seen that side of Jefferson before and—"

"Janine was right about this. I hate when that happens," Debbie muttered.

"Very funny."

"Honey," Debbie said on a sigh, "you're setting yourself up for a fall. I can hear it in your voice. You're going island girl on me here."

"No, I'm not." She took a sip of coffee, then broke off another piece of her scone. Nodding at the waitress who strolled past, she popped the pastry into her mouth, chewed and said, "I'm not stupid, Deb. It's not like I'm planning a pretty wedding or practicing signing *Mrs. Jefferson Lyon* on my notebook."

"I've got to go outside for this. Hold on a sec," she said, and a long moment of silence passed before she came back. "Sorry. But I just don't feel comfortable yelling at one of my best friends when everyone in the office can overhear."

Caitlyn should have been grateful. The travel agency

Debbie owned and operated was a busy one. "I don't need to be yelled at, thanks."

"No, what you need is a swift kick in the memory. But since I'm not close enough, this'll have to do," Debbie said.

Caitlyn's eyes rolled as she broke off another piece of scone.

"Cait, honey, Jefferson Lyon is bad news. He's too rich. Too powerful. Too used to getting his own way."

Caitlyn winced a bit. Debbie's erstwhile fiancé had also been rich, powerful—and, oh, yeah, a bigamist.

Before she could say anything, though, Debbie was talking again.

"Jefferson is *not* what he's pretending to be. Only a few days ago you said yourself that he was up to something."

Scowling now, she pushed the plate of scones away, scrawled her name and room number on the check and stood up. Walking briskly out of the restaurant, she headed for the bank of elevators on the far side of the lobby.

"I really hate it when my friends use logic," she muttered and jabbed the up button. While she waited, she said, "But maybe he's changed—and, man, that sounds so movie-of-the-week. He hasn't changed, has he?"

"Nope," Debbie agreed. "Remember when you said that Jefferson is only concerned with one bottom line? His own?"

"Do you take notes when I talk or something?" Caitlyn demanded, only half joking. "It's really hard to argue when someone keeps using your own words against you."

"Good."

She stepped into the elevator and punched the button for her floor. Ignoring the older man entering right behind her, she said, "Fine, fine. You're right. But, Debbie, when he kissed me, he—" She stopped, glared at the man listening with avid interest and lowered her voice. "I swear, I felt something from him. Something real. Something…"

"Hard and horny?" Debbie provided.

Caitlyn's head smacked against the wall of the elevator. She didn't want to believe her friend. Didn't want to think that Jefferson could kiss her like that and feel nothing but a physical response. But then again, this was the man *People* magazine had called one of the most eligible bachelors in the country last year.

And not only had Jefferson had the damn article *framed,* he'd made a vow to be on that list every year for the next twenty years. This was not a man who wanted to end his days of solitude. He wasn't looking for a permanent relationship. And if he were, he wouldn't be looking at Caitlyn.

His kind of man wasn't interested in women like her. He went for the models, the actresses, the blue-blooded East Coast beauties.

If he was making a play for an admin from Long Beach, there had to be a reason.

The elevator pinged and the doors opened slowly. She stepped out, said goodbye to Debbie and walked down the hall to her room. If she was a little disappointed by the realization that there was nothing real between her and Jefferson, she'd get over it. It's not as if she had really believed everything he'd said to her. Not that she'd actually toyed with the idea of something real between them.

Okay, fine, she thought with a disgusted sigh. So she'd done a little bit of toying.

She swiped her key card, pushed the suite door open and paused when she heard Jefferson's voice saying her name.

"Caitlyn is falling right into line," he said, clearly on the phone. "I'm telling you, Jason, it's going to work."

Falling right into line? Caitlyn scowled and focused on what else he was saying to Jason. The younger of the Lyon brothers, Jason had turned his back on the company his grandfather had founded and gone into medicine. Now he was an emergency-room doctor outside Seattle.

"You don't understand, that's all," Jefferson was saying. "I know what I'm doing."

And just what exactly *was* he doing?

Caitlyn glanced down the long hallway to make sure no one could see her hovering outside her own room, eavesdropping. Assured the coast was clear, she frowned again, leaned in and listened to every word.

"I'm telling you she's ready for it. I know what you said, and if I had the time, maybe I wouldn't be doing it this way. But, damn it, Jas, I need her at work. She knows the specifics on every deal we've got coming up in the next six months. I don't have time to train someone else."

He paused and Caitlyn's hand tightened on the doorknob. She gritted her teeth to keep from hissing.

"The seduction of Caitlyn is moving along great. I should have her back to work within a week or two."

She narrowed her eyes on the door as if she could stare right through it and bore a hole through Jefferson's thick head. That's what he'd been up to all along, she thought. Seducing her, romancing her, all to get her back to work for him.

"I know what I'm doing," he said, his voice dropping low enough it was hard for Caitlyn to hear over the pounding of her own heartbeat. "I get her into bed, get her home to Long Beach, then I act like a bastard and get her to break up with me. Then she'll feel so bad about dumping me, she won't have the heart to quit working for me, too."

Her jaw dropped and her eyes narrowed. *Unbelievable.* Did he really think she was that stupid? That malleable?

"It is not a stupid plan," he argued.

Thank you, Jason, she thought furiously.

"I don't have stupid plans. And, little brother, you know as well as I do that when my mind's made up on something, I never lose."

Until this time, Caitlyn vowed. This time he would lose. This time the world wasn't going to spin just the way Jefferson Lyon expected it to. She'd twist his idiotic plan around until she had strangled him with it.

Of all the nerve.

Of all the arrogant, self-serving… She just didn't have enough insulting adjectives to fit him!

"Right. I'd better go. Going to talk her into an early dinner, then a moonlight swim. Trust me, Jas, she'll go for it."

Caitlyn's hand fisted around the strap of her purse so tightly she wouldn't have been surprised to see the leather fused to her skin. But she took a deep breath, eased the door closed and winced as the lock snicked into place.

Then, making plenty of noise, she slid her key card through again and pushed the door open.

He was standing beside the closet and turned a wicked thousand-watt smile on her. If Caitlyn hadn't heard that little phone conversation between him and his brother, chances were her knees would have been melting again.

As it was, everything in her was cold and still.

Well, except for the seething rage.

"There you are," he said, drawing her into the room and taking her purse and packages from her. "I was about to send a search party to the village."

"Oh, you were worried?"

He stepped closer, ran his fingers up and down her arm and then brought her hand up to his lips. Planting a kiss on her fingers, he looked deeply into her eyes and asked, "What do you think?"

Wouldn't she love to tell him exactly what she was thinking? Wouldn't she love to turn him out on his ear? Make him sleep in a pool chair or something, as Janine had suggested earlier in the week. She'd love to see surprise on his face when she called him on his plan. She'd love to see him try to talk his way out of what she'd heard.

But as satisfying as all that sounded, she had a better idea. He had a plan to seduce her? Well, two could play at that game. She was going to turn all of this around on him. Caitlyn was going to seduce *him*. She was going to go along with his scheme, let him think he was winning and then, just when he was flushed and pleased with himself…she'd dump his fine ass and quit.

Again.

And there was no time like the present to start. Swallowing the fury still choking her, Caitlyn pulled her hand free of his and forced a shy, sweet smile.

"Didn't mean to worry you," she said, and turned, scowling, to pick up her packages. When she faced him again, that smile was in place and her voice was even, soft. "I thought, if you wanted to, we could have an early dinner. Maybe take a swim?"

His eyes narrowed and she wondered if maybe she'd played her hand too quickly. But then his expression smoothed out and he was giving her that knock-'em-dead smile of his. "Exactly what I was thinking just a minute ago."

"Isn't that a coincidence?" she said, and only mentally added, *You are so busted, Jefferson. And you're going to be so sorry you messed with me.*

At the door to the bathroom, she paused and looked at him. "I'm going to take a shower, get ready. Won't take me long."

"Great. I'll just make a few phone calls while I wait."

She nodded and closed the bathroom door. Leaning back against it, she wondered if he'd call Jason back. Tell him that the plan was working. Tell him that good ole Caitlyn was, as he had put it, falling right into line.

Caitlyn dropped the bags onto the white-tiled floor and leaned on the wide sweep of blue counter to stare at her own reflection. Her skin was tanned a bit from all the days in the sun. There were subtle highlights in her hair and sparks of fury in her eyes.

Keeping her voice low, she talked to her own image as if that reflection needed reassuring. "I've been resisting his advances for all the right reasons—but he's been making those advances for all the *wrong* reasons. Well, it's time he learned a lesson."

Dinner was great. Even better than he'd hoped. He'd arranged for the private table again and between the moonlight, the candlelight and the ocean breeze, he couldn't have ordered up a more romantic evening.

Now, as they walked along the sand, he saw Caitlyn was clearly enjoying herself. In fact, she seemed more open somehow to him. More affectionate. All to the good, he told himself, despite the twinge of conscience struggling to rear its ugly head.

His brother, Jason, had been wrong when he'd said, *Using Caitlyn like this is going to backfire.* Jason didn't understand. He wasn't using Caitlyn. He wasn't doing this only for himself, after all. It was for her best, too. She loved her job. She was good at it. And she'd quit without thinking it through. She'd be glad to be back where she belonged.

"The beach is practically deserted," she said, and her voice was so soft the warm wind nearly carried it away.

He shrugged but reached for her hand. Folding his

fingers around hers, he said, "There's some dance competition tonight in the main club."

"Well, I'm glad. A moonlit beach is better when it's empty." She turned her face up to his and smiled, and just for a second Jefferson's breath caught in his lungs. The shine of starlight was in her eyes and a pale wash of moonlight bathed her skin in an ivory glow.

She wore a summery dress with her bathing suit beneath it, and he suddenly wanted to see her in that bikini of hers again. In the daylight, at the pool, her body was warm and tanned and curvy. He wanted to know what all that soft skin looked like in the softer light of the moon. He wanted to touch her. To feel her reach for him, arch into him.

He wanted to kiss her again.

Fine. He could admit, at least to himself, that he'd been doing a lot of thinking about that kiss they'd shared. At the unexpected heat of it. Of the warm rush of something wild and tender that had pulsed inside him as she'd breathed into his mouth.

At last, when the brightly lit resort was far off in the distance, a smear of light in the dark, they stopped. Jefferson pulled two wide, plush towels from the bag he'd been carrying and spread them on the sand while Caitlyn watched. She kicked off her shoes and then turned her back to him.

"Help me with the zipper?"

He smoothed his fingertips across her back, dipped them beneath the soft cotton fabric of her dress and slowly pulled the back zipper down. She looked up at him over her shoulder and gave him a brilliant smile that punched into his stomach like a fist.

"Thanks." Then, shaking her hair back from her face, she said, "I'm going for a swim. You coming?"

He watched her turn and run into the water, her long legs kicking through the waves that crested on the shore, sending spray flying through the air. His gaze locked on the curve of her behind, the narrowness of her waist, the elegant sweep of her arms as she lifted them to the night sky.

In a flash that took only seconds, his body went hard and hot and needy. Want pooled in his belly and reached up to grab at the base of his throat. Jefferson stripped out of his clothes and followed after her, unable to take his gaze from her. Unable to think about anything but reaching her, touching her, holding her.

He ran to the water's edge and kept moving until he could dive into the oncoming surf. The warm tropical water surrounded him as he breached the surface and swung his hair out of his eyes. Spotting her just a few yards away, he swam to her and she smiled as he got closer. Moonlight was on her. In her. Shining from her eyes, dazzling her skin.

And his slow seduction went completely out of his head. He only knew he had to have her. Now.

"You're beautiful," he said—and was as surprised as she looked to find that he really meant it. Why had he never noticed before now?

How had he looked at her every morning for three years and not noticed the curve of her jaw, the depth of her eyes, the kissability of her mouth? He didn't know. Didn't care. All that mattered was the moment at hand.

He cupped her face in his palms, lowered his mouth to hers and tasted. Feasted. She rose up on her toes and the motion of the warm water surrounding them pushed her against him. He held her tightly, arms around her waist in a grip that defied anyone to try to pull her from his grasp.

Electrical-like charges sparkled in his veins and he felt the rush of need clawing to be freed. Again and again, he took her, his mouth plundering hers, taking as well as giving. He heard her sigh, felt the groan rippling up her throat and luxuriated in the sound.

She fed his need, and when her arms came around his neck and pulled his head down harder, more firmly to her own, Jefferson's blood pumped hard and fast. He shifted, holding on to her with one arm, keeping her steady as the ocean lazily rocked them in a warm, soothing embrace. And he slid his free hand down her body, along her curves and down to the strip of fabric riding low on her hip.

Sliding beneath the edge of her white bikini, his fingers moved unerringly to the one spot he most craved to touch. To stroke. He found her heat and dipped inside. One finger, then another, sliding in and out of her tight center until she pulled her mouth free of his, tipped her head back and gasped for air like a woman drowning in sensation.

"Jefferson!" His name tore from her throat in a deep, rumbling groan.

"Let me," he whispered, dipping his head to the hollow of her neck. Kissing, nibbling, running the edges of his teeth across her skin. He tasted her pulse, found it battering furiously in her veins and knew she felt what he did. Knew she wanted as badly as he did. And knew he couldn't wait much longer to have her.

His fingers moved in and out of her hot sheath, setting a rhythm she strived to match. Her hips rocked with him, into him. She opened her thighs and hooked her legs around his middle, giving him deeper access. His thumb brushed at one sensitive spot, and he felt her shiver, heard her whispered intake of breath.

"So hot." He breathed the words against her skin, moving his mouth up the length of her neck. Kissing her jaw, her cheek, her mouth again, loving the taste of her. "So right."

She held on tightly now, her hands sliding over his water-slick back, her nails scraping his skin. She leaned back, arching into him, riding his hand with an abandon he wouldn't have expected from the woman he had always considered the ultimate in tidy efficiency. He gave her what she needed, what they both needed. His fingers stroked and caressed and delved deep within until he felt the first ripple of her climax begin to overtake her. And then he took her mouth with his again, his tongue claiming hers as she whimpered with the staggering force of the orgasm he gave her.

When she was spent, he swept her into his arms and carried her from the ocean. She speared her fingers into his hair and kissed him, secure in the circle of his arms. She leaned into him, pressing her breasts to his chest, kissing him, giving him everything she had.

Quickly he laid her down on the towels spread on the still-warm sand and just as quickly pulled her bikini off and tossed it aside. Moonlight was all she wore now and it graced her curves, her skin, like an ivory cloak. She lifted her arms to him and said, "Now, Jefferson, I want it all now."

He stripped off his own bathing trunks, stretched out beside her and allowed himself the sheer pleasure of touching her all over. He dipped his head to her breasts and one after the other he took her dark, hardened nipples into his mouth. She groaned again as he suckled her and he felt the magic of her pouring into him.

Her every sigh inflamed him. Her every breath urged him on. She moved beneath him, and his body tightened until he felt as though he were going to explode, shatter. He shifted over her, needing completion, needing to feel himself held within her.

She parted her legs for him and met his first thrust with a lift of her hips that took him deep inside her heat. He felt her acceptance, felt her welcome and lost himself in the fire building between them.

Again and again they came together in the pale shadows. With whispered words and half-muttered sighs, they became the rhythm that pulsed between them. With the stars overhead and the faint sound of music drifting to them from far away, Jefferson stared down into her wide brown eyes and felt himself drowning in their depths.

Eight

Caitlyn told herself it was a victory. She hadn't been used. She had been the one doing the using.

But the victory was an empty one and she knew it. She'd expected to have sex with him, enjoy herself and move on. Put him firmly and completely behind her. But since her body was still humming and her heart was racing frantically in her chest, she knew now that had been a big mistake.

She stared up into his eyes and felt her heart turn over. Strange, she'd heard that expression most of her life and until now she'd always thought it was just that: an expression. Now she knew there was more to it than that.

She was in love with Jefferson Lyon.

A man who couldn't be less interested in her.

Just perfect.

"Aah," he said, easing himself to one side of her, gently disentangling their bodies. "That was…"

"Amazing?" she offered in a chipper voice despite the cold emptiness she felt at his absence. "Wonderful? The earth moved?"

He propped himself up on one elbow and looked down at her. His eyes were filled with shadows, making them all but impossible to read. And maybe, Caitlyn thought, that was for the best.

"All of the above," he said, then paused and added with a wince, "plus…unprotected."

That gave her a quick jolt. Stupid to have not thought of that. No excuse, really.

He shoved one hand through his wet hair as he shook his head in self-disgust. "That's never happened to me before," he admitted. "I've never lost control like that. Look, Caitlyn, I wasn't thinking. I can apologize, but that won't do either of us any good."

"It's all right." The words forced themselves past the knot in her throat. Sitting up, she reached for the dress she'd torn off only a few minutes ago. "I mean, it was stupid. Of both of us. But as long as you're healthy, you don't have to worry about pregnancy or anything. I'm on the pill."

"I am," he said. "Healthy, I mean."

"Then, there's no problem, is there?" Except, of course, for the gaping open wound on her heart. But that wasn't his problem; it was hers.

Standing up, she stepped into her dress, pulled it up

and struggled with the back zipper. In a flash, he was standing behind her. His fingers brushed against her skin, sending tingles of sensation rippling through her as he zipped up the dress.

"Thanks." She heard him getting dressed but didn't turn around. Didn't watch him. Damn it, what was she supposed to do now? It was on the tip of her tongue to tell him she knew all about his childish plan to trick her back into working for him. She wanted to face him, see his eyes when he realized that she had *known* how he'd planned to use her.

But something stopped her.

Call it foolish. Hell, call it stupid. But it was there. The urge to keep quiet. To just go along with his plan, let him think it was working. Let him think he'd lulled her into believing he wanted her. There was time enough to disabuse him of the idea. She could face him down later with the stinging truth.

And then maybe it wouldn't feel so raw to her. Maybe then she'd be feeling less hurt and more righteously indignant.

He turned her around and pulled her into his arms. Silently, she went into his embrace, laid her head on his chest and listened to the steady thump of his heart. His arms cradled her, his chin rested on top of her head. When he released a long breath, it almost felt to her like a sigh.

Which just went to prove that her heart was too easily led at the moment.

"I don't know what to say to you," he whispered, still

holding her, standing there quietly as if he could hold that position all night and not want anything else.

He was good, Caitlyn thought with a pang. She'd never really given him the credit he deserved. No wonder he always had women draped all over him. His touch, his words, the heavy sighs. The man was a consummate actor. He almost had her fooled, despite knowing the truth.

"Don't say anything," Caitlyn said, and meant every word. She didn't want to hear any more lies. Not now. Not when everything she was feeling for him was so tender. So easily bruised.

"I want to, though."

No, don't, she thought but knew he wouldn't keep silent. Knew that if he was going to play his role well, now he had to tell how much he cared for her. To set the stage, so to speak. To keep her soft and gooey for him— and, oh, how it infuriated her to know that if she hadn't heard that phone call of his, she would have been just what he was expecting.

He shifted her in his arms, drew back slightly and lifted both hands to cup her face. His thumbs smoothed across her cheekbones and his gaze moved over her with a caress as palpable as a touch.

"Being with you," he said, his tone soft, tempting, "was more than I thought it would be. It touched me, Caitlyn."

She felt the sting of tears and furiously fought them back. She wouldn't give him one tear. Wouldn't allow him to one day look back at this moment and think to himself what a fine job he'd done. Instead, she used his words to bolster her own defenses. To remind her that this was a man who was clearly willing to do whatever he had to to achieve his goals.

"Me, too," she said, and forced herself to kiss him briefly, lightly, before stepping out of his arms to give herself a chance to settle.

"Me, too?" he echoed. "That's all you've got to say?"

She glanced at him, noted the confusion on his face and took a sort of dark cheer from it. "It was great, Jefferson. You were great. But I'm cold now and I want to go back to the hotel."

"Oh." Nodding, he swept up their towels and bathing suits, shook out the sand and tossed the whole mess over his shoulder. Reaching out, he took her hand in his and gave it a squeeze. "Let's get back to the room, then. We can talk more there."

His fingers were warm and strong and just for a minute, she let herself pretend that they really were a couple. That their lovemaking had meant something. That there was a future for them beyond the comeuppance that Jefferson so had coming to him.

But when he smiled down at her with the patented Jefferson Lyon seduction smile, Caitlyn inhaled sharply. Her heart ached and she wondered if she was going to be able to play along with this after all. Despite being furious with him, she loved him. And dragging this out was going to be harder on her than it would be on him.

Yet…she knew she would play the game he had begun. Because, when it was all over, she would at least have some memories of them together.

Setting herself up for even bigger pain down the road? Probably. But at the moment, with her blood still humming and her body still tingling from his touch, it seemed a good enough trade-off.

Jefferson was having a great time. Well, not at the moment, as he had just gotten off the phone with Georgia, who could make any rational, sane man want to tear his hair out.

But on the whole, this time on the island had been good. He stood outside a village shop waiting for Caitlyn to come back to him and realized that he was actually enjoying himself.

The sun was hot, but the air off the ocean sifted through the heat, soothing him and everyone else on the brick-paved street. The air was spicy with the scent of the flowers lining the walkways and from somewhere down the street came the rhythmic sound of steel-drum music.

It had been years since he'd had a real vacation. And he was only just realizing how much he'd needed this break from the everyday world. But it wasn't just being away from work that felt so invigorating. It was Caitlyn.

She was fun. Exciting. And more alluring than he would ever have thought possible. He had no idea how he could have worked with her for so long and never noticed just how amazing she really was. She was different from every other woman he'd ever known.

Easy enough to understand, he reassured himself constantly. They had a real connection. A relationship that went beyond the bedroom. They talked and laughed about their families. She understood his work, his company, as well as he did. She had an adventurous spirit—always willing to try something new, something different.

Through her enthusiasm, she made him see everything around him in a new light. Ordinarily. he was a man who thought an hour away from his work was an hour lost. Now he looked forward to every damn day with her.

Together, they had taken surfing lessons—and watching her try time after time to stand up for more than a second, he'd felt admiration for her stubborn determination. They went parasailing behind a boat, and he would never forget the sound of her laughter as she danced in the wind beneath a rainbow-colored parachute. They danced in the resort's club every night, and when they went back to her room, they lay together in the wide bed.

He leaned one shoulder against a light pole and squinted into the sun, staring blindly at the people who passed him by. He was caught in some sort of weird place where all he wanted was for her to smile at him. For her to touch him and reach for him during the night. Night after night he held her, made love to her and woke next to her in the morning. Another first for him. Jefferson wasn't the kind of man who hung around after sex. He didn't like "morning afters" and had made a point of never having one of his women spend the night at his home.

But with Caitlyn he found he wanted to watch her

wake up. Wanted to be the first thing she saw when she opened those amazing brown eyes of hers.

And as the days passed, he began to worry about that. His plan was working all too well. Caitlyn was happy and he was sure to be able to smooth-talk her back to work. But the downside was he was getting too involved in the game himself.

Worse, he was beginning to wonder how the hell he'd do without her once they returned to the real world. Once he'd convinced her to "break up" with him.

"Why the frown?" Caitlyn asked as she came out of the candle shop carrying a red-and-white-striped bag.

"Nothing." Straightening up, Jefferson pushed his disturbing thoughts aside and automatically took the bag from her and dropped one arm around her shoulder. That move had become all too instinctive recently, but he wasn't going to worry about that at the moment. "Just thinking about work."

"Aah." She nodded, glanced up at him and asked. "Another call from Georgia, then?"

Jefferson sighed and bit back the irritation bubbling inside. The older woman was making him nuts. Yes, she was trying. He was willing to admit that. But every time she called him with a problem, she hemmed and hawed so much he could hardly understand her. Just one more reason to strengthen his resolve to keep Caitlyn at work.

"Apparently Hammersmith called the office today and wanted another discount on the shipping charges." Harvey Hammersmith, one of the accounts who'd been with the company since Jefferson's grandfather's time, was always trying to get discounts on the heavy equipment he had shipped from Taiwan. Harvey claimed it was the least Lyon could do since he was one of their oldest clients.

"He tries that every year," Caitlyn said, laughing, then paused and asked, "She told him no, didn't she?"

He sighed. "No, she didn't. Said she didn't want to take the responsibility. At least I think that's what she said between all the pauses and throat clearing and mumbling. She told him she'd see what she could do."

"But he already gets a hefty discount based on tonnage shipped."

"See?" he said, impressed with her all over again. "*You* know that. Georgia *should* know that."

"Georgia's nervous." She shrugged and tossed her thick, wavy hair back from her face. "I told you. Every time she has to speak to you her mouth goes dry."

An electric golf cart beeped its horn, and Jefferson looked over his shoulder, then steered Caitlyn out of the street and up to the sidewalk so the guy could pass.

"She can't do the job, Caitlyn."

"No, not the admin job, you're right," she said, and came to a stop. Facing him, she looked up and said, "You'll have to hire someone else for that. But Georgia does her own job very well."

"Except," he reminded her, "for little typos that could cost me four hundred million dollars."

"You're being too hard on her. You always are."

"And you're too nice." He stroked one finger down her jaw. "You always are."

She turned her face into his touch, then sighed a little. "Not always."

He frowned, wondering what it was he'd just seen flash in her eyes. Then she smiled again and he let it go. "When we get back to Long Beach," he said, "you can have her be your assistant, if you want. But, seriously, I don't want her dealing one-on-one with the customers anymore."

"Jefferson—"

"I know," he interrupted her neatly, bent down to plant a quick kiss on her mouth and then smiled. "You quit. I understand. But that's not to say I'm not going to keep trying to get you back."

She tipped her head to one side and looked at him. "And how far would you go to get me back?"

He grinned and fought down what might have been a twinge of conscience again. "As far as I had to, of course. You're one in a million, Caitlyn. I don't want to lose you."

"Right. Of course not."

"We're good together, Caitlyn," he said, pushing just a bit more. Wanting her to admit that the two of them made a good team. Needing her to at least acknowledge that much. He took her chin with his thumb and forefinger and grinned at her. "You can't tell me you don't enjoy running my life."

She slipped back and out of his grasp, and he thought he saw regret flash in her eyes before it disappeared as quickly as it had appeared.

"I don't know, Jefferson." She took a breath, blew it out and said, "I'll have to think about it. Okay?"

"Okay, no more shoptalk," he said, and hooked one arm around her shoulder again, drawing her close enough that she was tucked up into his side. "Let's get something to eat."

"Always a good idea."

They hadn't gone more than a few feet when she stopped again, caught by something in a display window. "How great is that?"

"What?"

She tapped her finger against the glass and pointed. "That bracelet there."

He'd done this before, Jefferson thought. Every woman he'd ever been with had always found a way to stop and peer in a jewelry store window. Usually, they'd home in on a diamond necklace. Or maybe some earrings. Not surprising that Caitlyn was doing it, too.

"Nice," he said, looking at the display of diamond and emerald necklaces spread out across blue velvet. Sunlight caught the stones and glittered in brilliant flashes.

"No," she said, and tapped the glass again. "Not the ones in the back. This. In front."

All that was in the front of the case was a simple sterling-silver charm bracelet. Surprised, Jefferson looked at her and then back at the simple piece of jewelry. Spread atop a mirror, just beneath the delicate links of silver were several different charms, all with detailed, delicate workmanship.

"You're talking about the charm bracelet?" he asked just to make sure. "Not the diamonds?"

"Well, yeah. See the tiny surfboard?" She looked up

at him, laughter in her eyes. "It's got a red stripe down the center. Just like the one you fell off yesterday."

He smiled at her, intrigued by a woman who saw silver charms in a window filled with diamonds. "I didn't fall," he corrected. "I jumped."

"Uh-huh. Whatever helps you sleep at night."

Her laughter was contagious. The light in her eyes was enough to warm a man down to the bone. And Jefferson felt something squeeze his heart. Something unexpected. Something a little disconcerting. He wasn't sure what to make of it, so he didn't try to explain it. Instead, he took her hand and led her inside the shop.

"Jefferson, you have to stop buying me things," she complained.

"Why?" he asked with a shrug. He liked buying her gifts. Liked how embarrassed it made her. Liked that she didn't seem to expect it. Every other woman he'd ever spent time with had had a greedy streak a mile wide. Not that he'd minded. A man didn't begrudge a few gifts.

But Caitlyn was something special. As he watched the jeweler attach the tiny surfboard to a link and then hook the silver bracelet around her slender wrist, he felt her pleasure like a shaft of something warm spearing through him. She was clearly more delighted with this simple gift than she had been with the topaz-and-emerald earrings he'd bought her the week before.

Holding up her arm, she smiled at the surfboard, then shifted her gaze to his. "Thank you, Jefferson. I love it."

And just for a second—one terrifying second—he wondered what it would have been like to hear her say *I love you.*

Nine

Caitlyn stared across the table at Jefferson and knew she wouldn't be able to keep up this pretense much longer. She looked at him, saw his smile, the shine in his pale blue eyes and felt her heart thump heavily in her chest. She had made such a huge mess of things.

Thank god Janine and Debbie would be arriving within the next couple of days.

She needed her friends to give her a swift kick in the butt. If she had told them about her stupid idea to turn Jefferson's seduction plan around on him, they would have talked her out of it. Which, she guessed, was exactly why she hadn't told them.

Every time the two women called now, she avoided the subject of Jefferson completely. Which wasn't easy since they both wanted to keep on top of what was happening.

But how could she explain to her friends when she didn't really understand it all herself? She'd gone into this eyes wide-open, with the idea of teaching Jefferson a much-needed lesson. To give him a little of his own back. To hurt him as he'd planned to hurt her.

The problem was she wasn't hurting him at all, but she was tearing herself up inside. Every day she spent with him only made her love him, want him, more than she had at the beginning of this really bad idea. Even though she knew he was only pretending to care, she had fallen for this relaxed, happy, affectionate Jefferson— and there was just no way out now.

Her mind wandered while he told her a story about his grandfather and she watched him smile with real fondness during the telling of it. And she wished that he felt something real for her. He was funny and smart and attentive and a fabulous lover. The perfect man.

If only it wasn't all a big, fat lie.

Idly fingering the tiny surfboard dangling from her charm bracelet, she remembered the day before, when he'd bought it for her. The look in his eyes when he'd realized she hadn't been drooling over diamonds had been almost laughable. Almost. Because it had just brought the truth crashing down on her.

Jefferson didn't see her for who she really was. To him, she wasn't even just another of the women he squired around. A woman to use for a while and then forget about. A woman who would be willing to accept a handful of diamonds instead of any real warmth. He'd expected Caitlyn to take her place in the legion of women he'd kept at a distance with high-priced gifts and smooth charm.

And when it was over for him, he expected that she would go back to work for him and life would return to the way it should be, according to Jefferson Lyon.

That was the moment when she'd finally accepted that she had to end this. Had to get Jefferson to go back home. She wanted some time with her friends. Time to get used to the fact that Jefferson was no longer going to be a part of her life.

"Hello?" He snapped his fingers in front of her eyes and Caitlyn jumped, startled. He grinned. "So where'd your mind drift to? Am I that boring?"

"Sorry," she said, and reached for her wineglass. Her throat was dry and felt thick and full with the promise of coming tears. She wouldn't cry in front of him. Wouldn't let him know that her plan had so fabulously backfired on her.

"Not boring at all. I was just…thinking."

"I can see that," he said, and his voice was low, nearly lost in the muffled hush of conversation that filled Fantasies' rooftop restaurant.

Overhead, the sky was black and dotted by stars. The moon dipped behind a swirl of clouds, turning the edges silver. Music played over the speakers, something slow and sultry and kept at a level that told Caitlyn the owner felt conversation was better when it wasn't shouted.

The place lived up to its name. Fantasies. She'd been

living one for the last week or so. With Jefferson in her bed every night and at her side every day. She'd indulged herself, enjoying every minute of their time together because she had known going in that it wasn't going to last.

Still, now that the end was on top of her, Caitlyn fought the urge to call Jefferson on the plan he'd concocted and she'd twisted. Was it so wrong to want one more night? Wouldn't tomorrow morning be soon enough to end the magic?

"You're doing it again. What're you thinking?" he asked, and reached across the table to cover one of her hands with his. "Looks serious."

She shook her head and concentrated on the feel of his hand atop hers. The smooth slide of warm flesh to flesh. The slight electrical hum of his touch. "No. Maybe I'm just tired."

"Not surprising." He grinned, then winced dramatically. "How far did we ride those bikes today? Eighty miles?"

Caitlyn laughed; she couldn't help it. Damn it, why did he have to be charming? Why did she have to love the shine in his eyes when he smiled? Why did he have to be such a liar?

Why couldn't he love her?

"It's only ten miles to ride around the whole island," she reminded him. "And we didn't go nearly that far."

"Felt like it," he admitted, then squeezed her hand. "But it was worth it to find that picnic spot."

"Yeah. It was beautiful."

An idyllic tropical garden, complete with waterfall, she remembered on a small sigh. It had felt as though they were the only two people on the planet. And when they'd stripped to go swimming in the crystalline water, she'd felt decadent.

Remembering what had come next—lying naked in the sun while Jefferson kissed every square inch of her body—made Caitlyn wish for more time with him. More time living this lie they were both playing at.

So what did that make her?

"We could go back tomorrow," he tempted.

Even if they went back tomorrow and the next day and the day after that, Caitlyn told herself firmly, it wouldn't change anything. They would still be caught in a web of lies. They would still each be wrapped up in their own schemes. None of it would be real.

None of it would mean anything.

She took a sip of her wine and blessed whatever friendly gods were watching when his cell phone rang, preventing her from having to answer him.

Frowning, Jefferson stared at the screen and muttered, "What the hell? This'll just take a minute." Then he opened the phone and said, "Max? How'd you get this number?"

Max Striver, Caitlyn thought with an inward smile. Good. Just the irritation she needed to keep Jefferson from going back to a conversation she didn't want to have.

"Georgia gave you my cell number?" Jefferson spoke through gritted teeth. His eyes narrowed in irritation and Caitlyn knew the older woman had just made another mistake. "Fine, then. What was so important you had to hunt me down?"

Whatever Max said to him wasn't good news, Caitlyn speculated. Jefferson's features tightened and she wouldn't have been surprised to see steam coming out of his ears. His tan made his pale blue eyes look almost silver and quiet fury sparked in their depths.

"How did you know that?" Jefferson demanded. "Aah. Georgia again. A veritable fount of information."

Oh, man. Caitlyn sighed in sympathy for Georgia. The older woman was so not scoring any points here.

A muscle in Jefferson's jaw twitched and he looked furious enough to throw his phone off the roof and into the ocean below. Instead, though, he took a deep breath and said, "Fine. Hold on."

"What's wrong?"

"Oh, nothing," Jefferson said, holding out his phone to her. "But maybe you could tell me why Max bothered to track me down just so he could talk to you?"

"Me?" she said, shaking her head. "How would I know?"

"Why don't you find out, then?"

He held the phone in a tight-fisted grip and the expression on his face said he wasn't amused. Well, Caitlyn thought, join the club. She took the phone, glanced at Jefferson, then said, "Max? Why are you calling me?"

"Aah, love, it's good to hear your voice," he said in a clipped British accent. Apparently, Max was completely oblivious to any undertones in Jefferson's voice. Well, either that or he simply didn't care. "You should have warned me that you would be resigning from Lyon Shipping."

Caitlyn squirmed a little under Jefferson's steely regard. Honestly, didn't she have enough trouble with one overbearing male? Did she really need *two*? "It was a spur-of-the-moment decision."

"And a wise one, in my opinion," Max quipped. "Imagine my desolation, though, when I called the office only to be told that you had left your job and gone on holiday."

"Yeah, it must have been wrenching," she said wryly, and tried a smile on Jefferson. She got a cold stare in return. This was going well. "Look, Max, whatever problem you've got, Georgia can handle it."

Okay, so she really couldn't, but the point was Caitlyn didn't work there anymore and *nobody* was paying attention to that one fairly important fact.

"Lovely woman, to be sure," Max was saying, and his words picked up speed. "But not the reason I'm calling."

"Then, why?"

"Why?" he repeated, clearly astonished she would have to ask. "To repeat my offer of employment, of course. Now that you're no longer working for Lyon, I'd like you to come to work for me. Executive assistant."

"Work for you?" she said, and instantly knew she shouldn't have. Jefferson went on red alert. Stiffening in his seat, he shot a glare around the crowded restaurant as if he could somehow send all the other customers into an alternate universe. Then he shifted his gaze back to her and it was Caitlyn's turn to squirm. "Max, I—"

"There's a lovely big raise in it for you," he said quickly. "Along with a company town house in Knightsbridge. Stay in it as long as you like, as long as it takes you to find where you'd rather live."

"Sounds great but—"

"Don't say no," Max said. "Not until you've given it some thought, in any case."

"Fine." Caitlyn kept her gaze locked on Jefferson's, watched temper flash and burn in those steely blue depths. "I'll think about it."

"That's all I ask, love. Now give me back to Jefferson, if you would."

She handed the phone over, but Jefferson simply snapped it shut without speaking. "He's offering you a job. Again."

"Yes," she said since it was pointless to deny it.

"Why didn't you tell him no?"

Irritation snapped inside her. "Why should I?"

"Because you work for me."

"No, I don't. Remember, Jefferson?" she prompted, feeling the beginnings of temper spark in her own blood. She felt like a flattened Ping-Pong ball. No one noticed that she'd been damaged…they just kept slapping her around with their paddles, expecting her to do what she'd always done. Roll along with no problem, despite the dents in her hide.

That was a stupid analogy but the best she could do under the circumstances.

Caitlyn had had enough. At least for the moment. She was tired of being the little trophy that Max and Jefferson grappled over. She wasn't a complete idiot. Max only wanted her to work for him because he wanted to steal her from Jefferson. And Jefferson only wanted her because she knew so much about his business.

No one really wanted *her.*

"You know what? I'm done. I didn't want to talk to Max. He called *me.* And now I don't want to talk to you." Standing up, she grabbed her purse, said, "Thanks for dinner" and stalked out of the restaurant.

She heard him call her name, but she didn't even slow down. Fury fed her steps. She passed dozens of interested faces as people watched her striding quickly across the tiled floor while Jefferson—the most controlled man she'd ever known—uncharacteristically shouted after her. But Caitlyn was beyond caring what the strangers around her—or he, for that matter—thought. At the moment, she only wanted distance. Both from Jefferson and from the situation.

She took the elevator to the ground floor and when the doors opened again, she hurried across the lobby, out the front walk and across the neatly tended lawn. Her steps were sure and fast. She paused only long enough to slip off her strappy sandals. Then, carrying them in one hand, she jumped over a low bed of asters and hurried down to the sand.

Music drifted from the rooftop restaurant. Moonlight dazzled the surface of the black water and a soft sigh of wind rolled in off the ocean and lifted her hair off her neck. The hem of her short black dress swirled around her, fluttering against her skin. The sand beneath her bare feet was still warm until she came close to the shoreline. And then the cool damp of it sneaked into her bones. Water lazed forward in small, steady waves, etching out darker patterns edged with the lace of foam.

She walked through the wet, kicking at the sand, spraying cool water into the air and trying to walk off the pain. The anger. The disappointment. Her chest felt tight, her lungs burned with every breath and her eyes were stinging with the threat of unshed tears. Grief warred with anger and slowly trumped it. Because at the very heart of things, she wasn't so much angry as disappointed and hurt. At least she was alone on the beach and that helped.

She should have known it wouldn't last.

"Damn it, Caitlyn, stop!"

His voice shouted over the pulse of the ocean's heartbeat didn't slow her down any. She didn't want to look at him. Once she did, she wouldn't be able to delay having the confrontation that was due them. She didn't want to end the lies with a moment of truth that would completely shatter the tidy little fantasy she'd been living.

His footsteps sounded out behind her, though, determined. When he grabbed her arm and spun her around, she instantly pulled free again. "Go away, Jefferson."

"I don't think so," he said, staring down at her as moonlit shadows danced across his features. "I want to know why you didn't tell Max no. Why you're stringing him along, letting him think you will work for him." His eyes narrowed. "Or is it that you're stringing *me* along?"

Caitlyn's jaw dropped. She looked up at him in absolutely stupefied shock. So, whether she'd wanted it or not, it appeared they were going to have this out here and now, anyway.

"Are you serious?" she asked, slapping her hand against his chest and giving him a shove that didn't budge him an inch. "You can really say that with a straight face? I'm stringing *you* along?"

"What do you call it, then?" He shoved both hands into his slacks pockets and glared at her.

"I call it playing your game, Jefferson." She inhaled sharply, deeply, and the night air filled her with the same shadows that surrounded her. "I call it trapping you with your own little scheme. I call it outwitting you."

"What the hell are you talking about?"

"I heard you on the phone with Jason last week."

He went completely still. His eyes cooled. "What are you talking about?"

"Don't even bother to try another pretty lie," she warned him. Then she had the satisfaction of seeing a quick flash of something that might have been regret move across his eyes and disappear again. Naturally, that regret was short-lived. Jefferson didn't make "mistakes." At least none he would admit to.

"You were going to seduce me, use me, then work it out so I dumped you. Then you figured I'd feel so bad about it that I'd go back to work for you."

His jaw worked, he blew out a breath, turned to look out at the ocean briefly, then shifted his gaze back to hers. One shoulder lifted in a halfhearted shrug and he scraped his hand across his face. "You weren't supposed to hear that."

"No," Caitlyn said, weary now with the games, the emotions, the lies. "I wasn't. I was supposed to *fall in line,* I believe is the term you used."

"I wish you hadn't heard."

"Oh, I'm sure of that, anyway."

"I didn't want to lose you," he admitted, his voice dropping to a low purr of a sound that rolled down her spine and threatened to weaken her resolve.

"So, instead, you used me."

Jefferson scowled at her choice of words but couldn't seem to find a way to dispute them. This wasn't supposed to be happening like this. She wasn't supposed to have known. And now that she did, he didn't have the time to come up with a way to work it to his advantage.

So, knowing the best defense was a good offense, he said, "Since you've known all along, I'm thinking you were doing a little using of your own."

"I just wanted to catch you in your own game."

"Congratulations, then. It worked."

"Did it?"

He laughed shortly and felt the harsh scrape of it in his throat. "You're not going to try to pretend you didn't enjoy yourself."

"No," she said softly, and he watched her eyes briefly close over whatever emotion was churning through her. "No, I'm not. But it's over. The game's ended."

She walked past him, headed back to the hotel. She

didn't look back at him, and damned if Jefferson was going to stand there looking after her. But when he caught up to her, she stopped and glared down at the hand he'd lain on her forearm.

"Let me go."

He didn't. His fingers locked around her arm and he felt the heat of her skin seep down deep inside him.

"It's over, Jefferson. Just lose graciously."

"I don't lose," he said tightly, staring down at her until his will alone forced her to meet his gaze. "You better than anyone should know that about me."

"Sometimes you don't have a choice."

"There's always a choice."

"And I already made one," she reminded him. "I quit. I don't work for you. We both know we're not a couple. So now my choice is to go back to my room and be *alone.*"

He tried a smile, since it was pretty much all he had left. "It's my room, too."

"Not anymore."

The hurt in her eyes tore something inside him. He actually felt it rip, but he wasn't sure what the hell it was. Couldn't have been his heart, since his heart hadn't been involved in any of this. But he hadn't meant to hurt her. Only to get her back. Prove to her how important she was to him. To the company.

"Leave me alone, Jefferson." She tore her arm from his grasp and walked off into the shadows, headed back to the bright lights of the resort.

Fine.

He'd let her go. For now. He wasn't going to chase after her. He was Jefferson Lyon and he chased *no one*.

He'd give her tonight to cool down.

Tomorrow, he'd have his say.

Ten

"What do you mean, there are no rooms available?"

The clerk at the registration desk lifted both hands and shrugged helplessly. "What can I tell you? We do have a room opening tomorrow, but…"

The resort lobby was still full of people despite the late hour. There were guests gathered around the low glass tables, laughing, having a drink. The hotel staff bustled, everyone busy. And the vague, generic music pumping through the speakers was beginning to give Jefferson a headache.

He grabbed the edge of the glass reception desk and leaned across. "Let me just remind you that I've been buying up your empty rooms for a week. And now I want one of them."

"Sorry, man." The younger man winced, then corrected himself. "I mean, sir. Yes, you were paying for the rooms, but only until the registered guests arrived. The empty rooms are gone now. But, like I said, I can help you out tomorrow."

"And what good does that do me tonight?"

"Sorry, sir." He shook his head and shrugged again. Then he looked past Jefferson to the woman standing behind him. With the matter settled, he was ready to move on to new business.

Perfect.

Jefferson pushed away from the registration desk and crossed the lobby, headed toward the elevators. Since Caitlyn had flounced away from him on the beach, he'd been alone, trying to think of a way to salvage the situation. He hadn't come up with a thing yet.

But he would. There was always a way.

He stabbed the elevator button, stepped inside when the doors opened and punched the floor number. "I'll just explain to her that there are no other rooms available," he told himself in the mirrored door. "She's a perfectly reasonable woman. It'll be fine."

No, he thought grimly, avoiding his own reflected gaze as if by doing so he could avoid the truth. It wasn't going to be fine. She was pissed, and he knew from experience that a pissed-off Caitlyn was not something to be taken lightly.

The elevator doors opened and he stepped into the hall. Turning left, he instantly spotted the suitcases standing outside her door. Irritation sputtered and slapped at him. His steps quickened and he rode his temper all the way down the well-lit hallway.

Barely glancing at his bags, he rapped three times on the door and waited for her to open it.

"Go away."

Her voice was muffled, coming through the heavy door, but her point was all too clear. "Open the door, Caitlyn. We have to talk."

"Oh," she said, and he heard her fingernails tapping against the door in an angry tattoo of sound, "I think we've already said plenty. Go away."

"I can't," he muttered, and lifted his head to glare at the couple who stepped out of their room and stared at him as if he were some psycho stalker. The woman took her husband's arm in a firm grip, and Jefferson was forced to admit that perhaps glaring at them hadn't been the right move. Instead, he forced a tight smile and said, "A little disagreement with my wife."

The woman still didn't look convinced, but her husband shot Jefferson a sympathetic smile. When they'd gone farther down the hall, Jefferson once again leaned into the door. "Damn it, Caitlyn, open up. I don't want to have this discussion in the damn hallway."

"I don't want to have it at all," she countered.

Voice muffled or not, her intentions were pretty clear.

He slapped one hand against the door. "There are no rooms. I don't have a place to stay tonight. Just let me in. We'll talk this through and—"

"Go sleep in a deck chair, Jefferson," she interrupted, and this time she must have been shouting because he had no trouble at all hearing her. "You're not coming back into my room and I don't care where you sleep. Is that plain enough for you? Do you need me to draw you a map?"

Fury pumped and he actually saw red at the edges of his vision. No one. No one had *ever* treated him like this and he damn well didn't care for it. His back went up and he swore he could feel every nerve ending in his body sizzling with insult. "You're serious, aren't you?"

"Give the man a prize!" She slapped the door hard to underscore her words, then told him again, "Go away. Before I call security."

"Security?" Astonished, he gaped at the closed door. "You wouldn't do that."

"Try me."

Eyes narrowing, mouth twisting in a scowl of pure frustration, Jefferson considered calling her bluff. He was in the mood for a showdown. But almost as soon as he thought it, he let the idea go. He didn't need the extra hassle of explaining the situation to an overworked security guard. Plus, he'd be damned if something like this would be leaked to the press. All it would take is some reporter looking for a nugget of a story and some hotel employee looking for some extra cash.

Nope, he told himself as he bent to scoop up his bags. He'd have this out with her tomorrow. To let her know, he leaned into the door again and said, "This isn't over, Caitlyn."

Caitlyn sat up most of the night, waffling between misery and rage.

She wondered where Jefferson was spending the

night, then told herself it shouldn't matter. She wondered if he missed her and then reminded herself that she was no more important to Jefferson Lyon than a top-grade copier.

The earrings he'd given her hung cold against her neck, and she told herself that they'd meant nothing to him. She touched the silver surfboard charm and wished it had all turned out differently.

Wished she hadn't cared.

Wished she'd never come to Fantasies.

But it was too late for wishes, she thought as she watched dawn begin to paint the sky. And far too late to change the way she felt.

"Isn't this interesting?"

Jefferson muttered in his sleep, opened his eyes warily and squinted into the rising sun. A man stood alongside his "bed" for the night—a surprisingly lumpy chaise. With the dawn behind him, the man was nothing more than a black silhouette, and it took Jefferson a minute or two to make out the guy's features. When he did, he knew things had just gone from bad to worse.

"What the hell are you doing here?"

Max Striver grinned, tucked his hands into the pockets of his slacks and rocked back on his heels. "Enjoying the view, for one," he said cheerfully. "The great Lyon, spending the night outside in a deck chair."

This was just great. Not bad enough that he'd had a total of about fifteen minutes' sleep, tossing and turning on the damn torture device. Added to that, his fitful sleep had been filled with dream images of Caitlyn's face, her eyes glittering with disappointment and anger. Apparently, though, the karma gods weren't quite finished with him.

No, he'd had to wake up to this.

"It's a chaise," he pointed out in what was barely more than a grunt.

"Aah. I stand corrected."

Jefferson groaned as he moved to sit up and his back ached like a bad tooth. In fact, every inch of his body hurt. The chaise was too short and too narrow and too lumpy and it had been damned cold in the middle of the night, too. What kind of tropical weather was that?

"If you're going to stand," Jefferson told him, "stand somewhere else."

"Is that any way to greet an old friend? Especially," Max added, "when you look like you could use one?"

He felt like an old man. Wincing, Jefferson rolled his head and heard his neck crack. Probably going to be twisted up like a pretzel for days. All because Caitlyn had been unwilling to see reason.

Lifting his gaze to Max, he demanded, "What're you doing here?"

"Well, as it happens," Max said, smiling as his gaze moved over the pool area of the plush resort, "I've decided I, too, needed a holiday."

The resort was beginning to wake up. The early morning crew was hurrying around the pool area, straightening, getting things ready for another busy day in paradise. And from somewhere, Jefferson thought with a covetous groan, came the scent of fresh coffee. But before he could get to it, he had to get rid of Max.

"A holiday. Uh-huh. So, of course, you had to come *here.*"

"All the best people do, apparently." Max kicked one of Jefferson's suitcases with the toe of his shoe and asked, "Having trouble finding a room, are we?"

His eyes narrowed into sharp blue slits. "I'm not in the mood for this, Max."

"If you were," the other man assured him with a smile, "this wouldn't be nearly so entertaining."

Jefferson pushed off the chaise and briefly thought about rolling the thing into the pool, just for spite. He felt like an idiot, sleeping on a pool deck. It was only worse being discovered by his oldest "friend." Despite their competitiveness, there had always been a thread of real comradeship between them. Maybe it was because their upbringings had been so much alike. Each of them was the eldest son of a wealthy family. Each of them destined to take over his own family's dynasty.

And in that, there was understanding, if nothing else.

Still, they'd done more arguing and competing over the years than hanging out together. And now was definitely not the time to start.

"You look like hell," Max offered, still so damned cheerful Jefferson briefly considered shoving *him* into the pool.

"Thanks for the update. And for stopping by." He tucked his shirt into his pants, raked his fingers through his hair and looked at Max as if trying to hypnotize him into leaving and giving Jefferson a little peace. Naturally it didn't work.

"Things not going so well with our Caitlyn, then, eh?"

"I don't know what you're talking about."

"Of course you do." Max laughed, nodded at the suitcases and guessed, "Your seduction technique failing you after all these years?"

There was a quick inward wince, but Jefferson ignored it. "What's that supposed to mean?"

"It means, I know you, Jefferson. Caitlyn quit her job and you followed her here. That can mean only one thing." Grinning now, Max said, "You set out to seduce her back. And by the look of it, you failed miserably."

Irritating as hell to be so obvious.

"You want to stay out of this, Max," Jefferson said tightly.

"Oh, I think not. You see, after having dispensed with you, I'm sure Caitlyn is ready for a man who won't see her as another piece of office equipment."

That stung. Not because Max said it but because, he thought with an inner groan, it was true. He had treated Caitlyn like that over the years. But it was her own fault. Being so bloody efficient. Trustworthy. Dependable. Was it his fault that he would go to any lengths to keep what he'd come to count on?

"And," Max was saying, "when I'm done sympathizing with her over your shameful treatment of her, I'll offer her that job again. Trust me when I say I know how to treat a valuable employee."

Rage nearly choked him. "You stay the hell away from Caitlyn."

One black eyebrow lifted. "You're in no position to be giving orders, Jefferson. I would think finding accommodation would be higher on your list of priorities."

"Don't worry about me."

"Oh, I wasn't. Not in the least."

Smug jerk, Jefferson thought and took another inner hit when he realized just how much like Max he himself was. Hadn't he, too, carried around that same sense of smugness? Hadn't he come here fully expecting to win Caitlyn over with some smooth moves and a few gifts?

No, they were totally different, he assured himself even though he didn't really believe it.

"You know," Max was saying now, "I've a deluxe suite waiting for me, if you need a place to freshen up…" He grinned again. "No, wait. Never mind."

"You're a real funny guy, Max," Jefferson said, bending down to snatch up his suitcases. "But guess what? I'm not enjoying the humor."

"If you were," his old friend told him, "I wouldn't be enjoying it half so much."

"Yeah? Well, find your amusement somewhere else." Jefferson pushed past him and walked across the tiled pool area, headed for the lobby—and hopefully a room. He'd reached the door when Max's voice followed after him.

"I'll just go check on Caitlyn, then, shall I?"

His friend's laughter chased him into the lobby and all the way to the registration desk.

By late afternoon Caitlyn had been ready to crawl the walls of her junior suite. She'd been locked up in her room since the night before, trying to avoid running into Jefferson. But there was only so much solitude she could take. She couldn't sleep, didn't have anything to read and wasn't interested in any of the in-room movies.

Besides, she thought, slipping into the seat Max Striver held out for her, why should *she* be the one to hide out? This was her vacation, after all. Jefferson Lyon hadn't been invited to join her. So why should she allow him the free rein of Fantasies while she cowered in her room?

"I do hope that frosty glare is really meant for Jefferson and not myself." Max grinned as he took his seat opposite her.

Caitlyn shook her head and made herself smile at the gorgeous Englishman. She'd been surprised to hear from Max when he'd called to invite her to lunch. But having him here was a nice distraction from her racing thoughts over Jefferson. Still, there was the question, "What are you doing here, Max?"

"Why does everyone ask me that question?" he wondered with a smile. Then he accepted the menus from a waitress and sent her away again with a regal nod. Handing one of the menus to Caitlyn, he said, "For the moment, I'm having lunch with a fascinating woman. Surely that's more than enough reason for my presence."

"To someone else maybe," Caitlyn said. Her gaze

moved over the elegantly scripted menu and didn't find a thing she was interested in. Her stomach didn't want food. It was tied into knots she was half afraid would never entirely disappear. Still, she had to eat something and the salad looked inoffensive. "But I know you too well."

His dark eyes flashed, his grin widened and one black eyebrow lifted. "Aah, there's no fooling you, is there?"

"No." Too bad Jefferson hadn't realized that.

The waitress came back, giving Max a thousand-watt smile and ignoring Caitlyn completely. Once they'd given their orders, though, the pretty girl disappeared and Caitlyn looked at the man opposite her. "So why not just tell me what you're up to, Max?"

"Fine, then, I shall." He braced his elbows on the table, met her gaze squarely. "I'm here to convince you to come to work for me."

"Max…"

"Hear me out now."

She nodded, but Caitlyn wasn't really interested. If she took the job, she'd have to move to London. Not bad on the face of it, but she'd have to walk away from her home, her friends. And even worse, as Max's assistant, she would still have to deal, occasionally at least, with Jefferson.

No, it wouldn't work.

She needed a clean break.

A new life.

"I can offer you quite an opportunity," Max was saying, and his voice took on the tone of a parent trying to wheedle a stubborn child. "Not just a substantial raise from what I guess Jefferson was paying you. But more variety in your work. As you know, Striver Industries is not involved only in shipping but in hotels and technologies, as well as a few other interesting side bits."

"It sounds great, but—"

"Now, now," Max said quickly. "Don't turn me down without at least thinking on it, Caitlyn. This could work out very well, indeed, for both of us."

"What could?" Jefferson appeared alongside their table. He glared at Max, who smiled affably back at him. Then that sharp blue gaze fastened on Caitlyn and she shifted under that cold, hard look.

"Jefferson," Max crowed quietly, "you look substantially better. Find a room, did you?"

"I did." He didn't look at Max again but kept his gaze on Caitlyn. "Why are you here with him?"

She did her best not to flinch away from the ice in his voice. "I'm having lunch. With a very nice man."

"To which you, my friend," Max reminded him, "have not been invited."

Jefferson continued to ignore him. Reaching out, he snagged a nearby chair, dragged it up to the table and sat down, turning toward Caitlyn.

She looked at him and felt her heart turn over. His eyes were shadowed as if he, too, had been awake most of the night. His mouth was a grim slash and his left hand was fisted on the table. He looked terrible, and, still, everything in her began to melt. Was it always going to be this way? God, she hoped not. She didn't want to live the rest of her life in pain.

But either way, that feeling only underscored the necessity of breaking away from Jefferson.

"Caitlyn," he said, ignoring the waitress who tried to offer him a menu.

"He won't be staying," Max assured the girl, and waved her off.

"Talk to me." Jefferson never looked away from Caitlyn and that was making it a little hard for her to breathe.

"I told you last night—we've said all there is to say," she murmured, and reached for her water glass. One sip helped ease the raw dryness in her throat.

"And then I find you here with Max."

"At a private lunch," Max futilely pointed out.

"Why are you with him?"

Why, Caitlyn thought, did she suddenly feel like a cheating spouse? For heaven's sake, she didn't owe Jefferson anything. She'd quit her job. He'd tried to use her. Stiffening her spine and gathering up the tattered threads of her pride, she said, "I'm here because he's offered me a job."

"Quite a good one, actually," Max said.

"And you're considering it?" Jefferson sounded appalled.

"I am." Caitlyn bit off the lie easily.

"Brilliant," Max said.

"You can't be serious." Jefferson leaned in toward her, his eyes glaring directly into hers as if he could see deeply enough that he would know if she were lying or not.

"Why shouldn't I take the job?" Caitlyn yanked her

white linen napkin off her plate and deliberately smoothed it across her lap. "I'm unemployed, remember?"

"Not any longer," Max reminded her.

"Stay out of this, Max." Jefferson shot the man a warning glare.

"No, *you* stay out of this, Jefferson." Caitlyn took a long, deep breath. "This has nothing to do with you."

"It has everything to do with me. You work for me. You know everything there is to know about Lyon Shipping." His blue eyes sparked with hastily banked fury. "If you go to work for the competition, there'll be a conflict of interest."

Caitlyn gasped. "You don't know me at all, do you, Jefferson? You actually think I would deliberately sabotage your company?"

He shifted in his seat, but the hard look in his eye didn't soften. "What else should I think?"

Max snorted. "If you want my opinion…"

"Max…" Both of them said his name in warning tones that had him lifting both hands and easing back into his chair.

"You're playing a dangerous game, Caitlyn," Jefferson muttered, and ignored the waitress as she delivered their meals. "If this is a ploy…if you're trying to get me to apologize, you've a long wait. I did what I thought I had to do. As I always do. As I always will."

Cold seeped through her and Caitlyn knew it was over. The fantasies, the dreams, the idle imaginings. She looked into Jefferson's cool blue eyes and felt the distance between them widen into a chasm that threatened to swallow her whole.

Carefully, as if she were made of glass and might shatter at any moment, she lifted her napkin, laid it alongside her uneaten lunch and looked at Max. "I'm sorry. I really can't stay. But thank you for the lunch offer."

Max nodded at her and fired a quick, hot look at Jefferson, who didn't even notice.

Caitlyn stood up, grabbed her purse strap off the back of her chair and gave Max a smile that cost everything she had. "And as for the job offer? Yes, Max. I will work for you."

"Excellent!"

Jefferson shoved out of his chair and looked down at her with ice glittering in his eyes. "You can't do that."

"I just did. Goodbye, Jefferson."

Eleven

Jefferson was only a step or two behind her as she headed through the restaurant, across the lobby and through the wide front doors. He caught up to her just as she stepped onto the neatly tended lawn. Grabbing her upper arm, he turned her around to face him.

Blood pumping, mind racing, he stared down into her dark, deep eyes and demanded, "Is this a joke?"

She looked down at his hand until he let her go, then she lifted her gaze to his. "I'm not laughing."

"In case you haven't noticed," he said tightly, "neither am I."

How had this all gone to hell so quickly? How had he lost control of the situation so completely? Jefferson Lyon was *always* on top of things. He never lost. He never came in second. And he *never* let a woman walk out on him.

And the thought of Caitlyn being the first was enough to make a cold, hard fist snatch at the base of his throat. He fought that feeling down and really reached hard for calm. Yet, even as he tried, her scent seemed to surround him, and he breathed deeply, drawing in that small part of her.

"Caitlyn," he said softly, watching the ocean breeze lift her hair off her neck, "you don't want to do this."

"I didn't once say I wanted any of this, Jefferson."

"Then, stop it here," he coaxed, and forced a smile he didn't feel. "Tell Max no. Come back to Long Beach with me."

She sighed and the pain in that small sound tore at him. "I can't work with you now, Jefferson. Not after…"

He knew what she was thinking. It was on her face. The regret. She meant she couldn't work with him after sleeping with him. So his little brother had been right after all. It had been a stupid plan. But it was too late to change that now. And even if he could, he wouldn't. He wouldn't give up the time he and Caitlyn had had together. It had become too important to him.

Now it was his turn to sigh. None of this was going as he'd planned. Nothing was turning out as it should. Stuffing his hands into his pockets, he stubbornly said, "It could still work."

"Of course you'd say that," she said, and one corner of her mouth turned up briefly. "But it's only because you don't want to give up. You don't want to admit defeat."

"Admitting defeat is what *makes* you defeated."

"Refusing to admit it doesn't change the facts," she said with a slow shake of her head.

He was losing. He felt it.

So he played his last card.

"Don't leave me for Max, Caitlyn."

"God, you still don't get it, do you?" She swung her purse off her shoulder and opened it up. Digging around in the cavernous depths, she said, "I'm not leaving you for Max, Jefferson. I'm just leaving you."

Her words stabbed at him and stole the last of his breath. Panic—a new and infuriating emotion—ripped through him, and Jefferson staggered under the impact. "Just like that. So easily. You can walk away without looking back."

"You think this is easy for me?" She laughed harshly and shook her head. "Of course I'll look back, Jefferson. And I'll see you. See what could have been. What might have been if you hadn't been too dumb to see it yourself."

Confusion rippled in with the irritation, the unfamiliar sense of imminent failure. "What're you talking about *now?*"

She pulled a small, neatly folded sack from her purse and held it out to him. He didn't take it.

"See," she said, "I thought I'd catch you at the game you were playing. Thought I'd use you as you'd thought to use me."

"Caitlyn…"

"But you're better at the game than I am. Way better. You managed to say all the right things, do all the right things, for all the wrong reasons. You kept the game going and never let it be real."

Pain tugged at his heart as he watched the sheen of moisture in her eyes, and he wanted to stop her. Wanted to tell her she was wrong.

But was she?

"The problem is," she said, picking up one of his hands and putting the small white bag in it, "it was real for me. I didn't mean to let it happen, but it did."

"What?" He glanced at the neatly folded bag before closing his fist around it. "What happened? What is this?"

"It's the jewelry you gave me," she said, blowing out a breath and straightening her shoulders with an obvious effort. "I can't keep it. Not now."

The earrings? The pearl necklace? The silver bracelet? She'd been so happy with them all. Enjoyed receiving them. Wearing them. And now she was just throwing them away? As if they were nothing? As if the week or more they'd had together was nothing?

"I wanted you to have these things," he argued. "We bought them together. You wanted this stuff. I know you did."

She chewed at her bottom lip and lifted one shoulder in a half shrug. "It's all beautiful. And, sure, I liked it all. But I didn't step into this game for the things you could buy me, Jefferson. It didn't matter to me. Never did. But those are the rules of the game you play. The rules you know. You buy gifts so you don't have to give anything of yourself."

Her words jabbed at him. Truth rattled inside him and demanded he recognize it. But he didn't. Couldn't. Besides, he'd given her more of himself in the last couple of weeks than he ever had to anyone else. Not that he'd had that intention in the beginning. It was only that it had turned out that way.

"So you didn't want anything from me." He nodded, shoved the damned jewelry into his pants pocket and felt it there like a hot rock. "You just wanted to—what?—get back at me?"

"That's how it started, yeah," she admitted. She shifted her gaze to look across the flower-strewn grounds, the achingly blue sky and the blistering sun pouring down on them. Finally, though, she looked back at him. "But it became something else. Something you want no part of."

"How do you know?" He grabbed her shoulders, held on, his fingers digging into her skin as if he could make her stay simply by getting a firm enough hold on her.

"Because I know you, Jefferson. And when I say I fell in love with you, you'll back away so fast there'll be sparks shooting off your heels."

He dropped his hands from her shoulders and stared at her in stunned silence.

"See?" She gave him a tired smile. "So just go, Jefferson. Let this be the one time that the great Lyon actually lost a battle."

She loved him?

And she could leave him?

Hell, if he was that easy to walk away from, how deep could this love she claimed to feel really be? "Fine. You go on. You go take a job working for Max. Move to England. Forget about me and my company."

"It's physically impossible for you to give up, isn't it?" Turning away from him, she started across the lawn and headed past the wide circular drive, where a cab was just pulling up. "I'll do it for you, then. I quit working for you two weeks ago. Now I quit loving you."

"Just like that?"

She stopped, turned and looked at him through those dark brown eyes that looked shadowed, wounded. "Just like that."

Behind her, the cab door opened and a tall woman with short, spiky brown hair stepped out. Seeing Caitlyn, the woman grinned and shouted a welcome.

"Janine!" Caitlyn turned and called her friend's name with relief, with pleasure. As the other woman came close, though, Caitlyn lifted one hand to hold her back before facing Jefferson again.

He ignored the other woman. Ignored the tourists coming and going down the wide flower-decked walkway. Ignored everything but the pair of deep brown eyes watching him. She was already too far away for him to reach. He could actually see her pulling away even as she stood there.

Love.

How had love come into this?

Why had she said it?

Did she mean it? Of course she meant it. Caitlyn didn't say things she didn't mean. But if she did love him…how could she just shut it off?

His insides twisted into knots and his fists clenched uselessly at his sides. This was new territory for him and Jefferson didn't have a clue what to do about it. All he knew for sure was that something precious to him was ending and he had to make at least one more desperate attempt to save it.

"If you walk away from me now, go to work for Max, I'll fire Georgia the minute I get back to Long Beach."

A long beat of silence stretched between them. A long enough moment for him to realize what he'd said and regret it. Yet, it was way too late to call it back, even if he had wanted to.

Caitlyn stared at him as if she'd never seen him before. "I can't believe you just said that."

"Believe it," he said, speaking around a knot of emotion choking him.

She laughed shortly, sadly. "How wrong can one person be about another, I wonder? I've known you a long time, Jefferson, and I never knew you to be so low. To take such a cheap shot."

He flinched under her steady regard but held his ground, no backup in him.

Shaking her head, she said, "You know what? You do what you have to do. I'm done."

He stood alone and watched her walk away. She linked arms with her friend, walked into the hotel and never glanced at him again.

And for the first time in his life, Jefferson Lyon felt like a first-class loser.

"Well, he's a jerk," Janine decided.

"Granted." Caitlyn leaned back against her headboard, grabbed one of the pale blue throw pillows and hugged it to her chest. "But for a couple of weeks he was *my* jerk."

"Damn it, Deb and I should have gotten here sooner," Janine muttered darkly. "Never should have left you alone with Jefferson Lyon for so long. I can't believe you had sex with him."

She couldn't believe it, either. For nearly two weeks, she'd fooled herself into believing that she could be close to Jefferson without getting emotionally involved. Now she knew that had been a huge mistake. But even knowing how it would end, she had the feeling she'd have done it all over again.

Because for a little while there'd been a real connection between them. Even if Jefferson could never admit to it. She knew he had felt it. Nobody was that good an actor.

"Well, I did."

"Was he good?"

Caitlyn shot her a look.

"Fine. Of course he was good." Janine sighed dramatically. "Creep. It's his loss, you know?"

"Not how it feels."

"I know, sweetie. But try not to think about him. Try to remember you're in an überplush place. With *me*." She grinned. "And Deb'll be here by tomorrow. And between the two of us, we'll get you feeling better again."

"Good. That'd be good." But Caitlyn doubted it. At the moment, she felt as though her insides had been hollowed out. Jefferson had packed and left the hotel less than an hour after their last confrontation.

Apparently, he'd finally decided to cut his losses. Would he really fire Georgia? No, she told herself firmly. Jefferson was a hard man, a ruthless businessman, but he wasn't a complete bastard.

"Yep," Janine was saying as she opened the minibar, looked inside and then slammed the tiny door shut again in disappointment. "What you need is another man. A big beach stud. Some uncomplicated sex. Relaxation."

"Oh, god." Caitlyn lifted the pillow to her face and held it there. When she spoke, her words came muffled against the fabric. "I so don't need another man."

"You know what they say," Janine said, and jumped onto the mattress beside Caitlyn, "when you fall off the horse…"

Caitlyn hit her with the pillow. "Jefferson's not a horse."

"Just a horse's ass?"

"Cute."

Janine flopped onto her back, folded her hands across her middle and stared at the ceiling. "I'm thinking that your vacation got messed up."

"That's not the only thing," Caitlyn muttered.

"*And,*" Janine continued, louder now, "now that the great one has oozed back home on his oil slick, it's time to put that world behind you, girl."

"I am."

"Oh, yeah. Doing a great job, holed up here in your room." Flopping onto her stomach, Janine gave Caitlyn's ribs a poke. "This is the ultimate spot, girlfriend. It's called Fantasies, not Hideaway. Come on. Get dressed. Wear something trashy and we'll go to the dance club and pick up a couple of studs with more good looks than brains."

Laughing, Caitlyn thanked heaven silently for a friend who knew just the right things to say. But despite Janine's good intentions, Caitlyn was in no mood for a distraction. Especially of the male variety.

"No, thanks. Think I'll stay right here and pout for tonight."

Janine's head dropped to the mattress. "Fine. We'll stay in. Order a couple of pitchers of margaritas and get plastered. Curse all men and their diabolical hold on women."

"A charming offer," Caitlyn said, and gave her friend a gentle shove, "but not necessary. My company stinks tonight, Janine. Why don't you go ahead? Go dancing. Relax. I promise I'll go with you tomorrow night."

"Yeah?" She lifted her head, narrowed her eyes. "You sure? I mean, if you want company, I'm your girl. We could—"

"Go." As much as she loved Janine, Caitlyn wanted to be alone. To soak in her misery and lick her wounds. She felt like hell and wanted to indulge in it a little. "Have a good time."

"Okay, if you're sure."

"Definitely."

"But you'll go out tomorrow night?"

"Yep."

"Okay, but no more crying over that idiot, okay?" Janine scooted off the edge of the bed, raked her hand through the messy spikes of hair. "He's not worth one more tear, Cait."

"I know," she said.

But when the door closed behind Janine, Caitlyn rolled onto her side, pulled a pillow in tightly to her body and let the rest of her tears fall.

Twelve

Jefferson didn't fire Georgia.

She quit.

He'd been back from Fantasies only two days when the older woman stepped into his office, dropped a signed letter of resignation on his desk and stood there primly, waiting for him to read it. When he had, he looked up and met her disapproving frown.

"You're quitting?"

"That's right."

He didn't even know what to say. He'd tried to be understanding. Patient. He'd given her a chance to take over Caitlyn's job temporarily and hadn't torn his hair out over her frequent mistakes. Hell, Jefferson had been silently awarding himself medals for his tolerance.

And *this* is the thanks he got?

Clearly, he didn't understand women.

"Why?" he asked, more from a twisted sense of curiosity than anything else.

"Because the job's no fun anymore."

"What?" Stunned, Jefferson just stared at the older woman.

She sighed and her already pinched mouth got thinner, tighter. "Since Caitlyn left, the morale of this company has gone downhill. You're never here. And when you are, you are distracted, abrupt, rude."

"Now, see here," he said, and stood up because he was beginning to feel like a third grader taken to task by a teacher.

"You're not the man your father was, Jefferson. And that, to my way of thinking, is a shame."

Anger churned inside him, but he held his tongue. Mainly, he thought, because she was right.

"Your father ran this company and raised a family," she was saying, and as she talked, her demeanor changed, shifting from disapproval to disappointment. "You and Caitlyn were a good team, you know. Without her, you're unfocused. Perhaps you'll be able to find another assistant to help you run your business. But," she added softly, "will you be able to find another woman who knows you so well and loves you anyway?"

Jefferson stiffened. "I don't know what you're talking about, Georgia, but—"

"Piffle," she said, and for the first time since he'd

known her, Jefferson realized she wasn't fluttering or stuttering or the least bit nervous. "If you don't know that girl loves you, you're a bigger fool than I thought you to be. Which, frankly, doesn't seem possible."

"Now just a minute…"

"I quit, so I'm free to say what I think," she reminded him with just a touch of vinegar. "It's really none of my business, of course, but you should go see Caitlyn. Before it's too late."

His chest felt as if it were in a vise. He could hardly draw breath. Ever since he'd left the resort, it had been this way. He hadn't been able to concentrate at work. And he found no sanctuary at his home, either. There was no place he could go where he didn't see Caitlyn's big brown eyes staring at him.

He couldn't sleep for dreams of her.

Couldn't think without hearing her voice in his mind.

Couldn't draw a breath without remembering the scent of her.

Then he remembered how she had looked when she'd told him to go away that last time. Shaking his head, though, he looked at the woman standing opposite him and said, "It's already too late."

Georgia smiled at him. "It's never too late to come to your senses, Jefferson."

When she left, he turned to the wide window behind his desk and stared out at the ocean. But he wasn't seeing the harbor. Instead, he saw blue-green water and Caitlyn diving into the waves. He heard her laughter peal in the air and felt her hands, soft on his skin. He felt the ache of arms that had been all too empty since leaving her and the hollow in his heart it had caused.

Was this love? Real love?

He hadn't expected it.

Hadn't, to be honest, thought himself capable of it.

Caitlyn had been such an integral part of his life, he'd taken for granted that she would always be there. And now that she wasn't, he could finally see just how important she was to him.

"Not too late, huh?" He plowed one hand through his hair as he walked across the room to the wall safe, hidden behind a painting of the Lyon company's first ship. Quickly dialing in the combination, he swung it open and reached inside for the small white bag holding the jewelry Caitlyn had returned to him.

He hadn't even looked at it since she'd handed it over. But now he opened the bag and poured its contents onto his desk. The earrings winked and glittered in the wash of sunlight and the pearl necklace seemed to glow like captured moonbeams.

But there was no bracelet.

No tiny surfboard charm.

Those she had kept.

Drawing his first easy breath in days, Jefferson told himself that maybe Georgia was right. Maybe it wasn't too late.

* * *

"This is amazing," Debbie said, and took a sip of her tall tropical drink. "Seriously, we should have done this years ago. Talk about the full-pamper treatment. I could learn to love this."

The three of them were stretched out on red-and-white-flowered chaises by the pool. The sun was warm, their drinks were cold and all was right with the world. Well, with their world, anyway, Caitlyn thought. For her, the sun didn't shine quite so brightly.

Janine snorted and pushed up on her elbows. Dipping her sunglasses down her nose, she looked at Debbie and grinned. "Don't be shy, Deb. Tell us how you really feel."

Caitlyn just listened to her friends. It felt good to be with people who loved her. And she hadn't actually thought about Jefferson in almost—she checked her wristwatch—five minutes now. That was an improvement, right? It would get better and better, a little each day, until eventually she might even convince herself that she hadn't really loved him. That she'd only been swept away by the passion and the surroundings.

"I'm just saying," Debbie countered, "it's good to let go. To just…be."

"Ooh. Zen now." Janine laughed again, reached for her drink, then looked at Caitlyn. "How're you doing?"

"I'm fine." When both of her friends only stared at her blankly, she insisted, "I am. Really. Better than fine. I'm great."

"Uh-huh." Debbie swung her legs off the chaise, sat

up and looked at her. "I know you don't want to hear this, Cait, but you need to move on, honey. There are lots of guys here up for grabs. Grab one."

"No, thanks." No other man was going to compare and she knew it. So why pretend differently? "I'm taking a man vacation for a while. But you go ahead, Deb."

"Well, you can't have mine," Janine said on a heavy sigh.

"You saw him again last night, didn't you?" Debbie asked. "Mr. Mystery. How come we haven't met him?"

Janine stretched like a satisfied cat and her mouth curled up in a slow smile. "Because I'm not ready to share."

"What's his name?" Caitlyn asked. "At least give us that much."

"I don't know his name," Janine admitted, and looked just a little embarrassed by the fact. "Ever since that first night I got here, when we met at the club…" She sighed heavily. "It was amazing. And unexpected. And totally out of character for me to just, you know—but, anyway, since then we just meet and…" She shook her head and grabbed her drink to try to cool off. "It's sort of sexier somehow, the not knowing each other's names. But, oh, god, he has this incredible accent and he's—"

"Accent?" Caitlyn echoed, wondering if somehow Janine and Max had found each other. "What kind of accent?"

"Sort of snooty British and—"

"Caitlyn?"

That deep voice reverberated through the air, ran up and down her spine and sent jolts of electricity zipping through her bloodstream. Was she hallucinating? *Nope.* The looks on Janine's and Debbie's faces told her that much. Both women looked ready to tar and feather somebody.

Slowly Caitlyn swiveled her head to look at the man standing at the foot of her chaise. "Jefferson?"

"Oh, no way," Janine started.

"You are so not welcome here," Debbie said.

He didn't look at either of them. His eyes were fixed on Caitlyn, and she could have sworn she actually felt the fire in his gaze licking at her skin.

"I need to talk to you," he said, his voice a low rumble of sound that seemed pitched exactly right to frazzle every nerve ending.

Not fair. She was doing her best to put him behind her. So not right for him to show up again and make it that much harder.

"Why did you come back?" Her voice sounded squeaky and she winced at the unevenness of it.

"I had to see you."

"Cait…" Janine's voice, worried.

"It's okay," she said, and a little shaky, stood up, feeling the cool tile of the patio beneath her bare feet. She grabbed her pale green cotton cover-up and slipped it on over her bathing suit. Then she tore her gaze from his long enough to look at each of her friends. "I'll be fine."

* * *

Jefferson felt the other two women glaring at him as he steered Caitlyn across the pool area and onto the garden path that wound its way to the beach below. He didn't blame them for being defensive. Hell, he knew what they thought of him and couldn't blame them for that, either. He hadn't exactly treated Caitlyn well.

But if she would give him a chance, he'd make up for that now.

"Your friends hate me."

"They're loyal friends," she said softly.

"I get that. But what about you?" he asked, walking beside her, content to feel the warmth of her brushing against him. "You hate me, too?"

"No," she said, and sounded tired. "I don't hate you. I just want to know why you're here, Jefferson."

"I want you."

"No more games." She stopped at the edge of the path, where the sculpted gardens gave way to the sand. The wind pushed her hair into her eyes, but she reached up with her left hand to swipe it back.

Smiling, Jefferson caught her hand and stroked his thumb across the sterling-silver bracelet and the tiny surfboard charm. "No," he said, smiling now because she was still wearing it. She still cared, whether she wanted to or not. "No more games. You kept this."

Embarrassed, she pulled her hand from his and lowered her eyes. "I forgot about it," she lied. "I was going to send it back to you—"

"No, you weren't."

"No," she said on a sigh. "I wasn't. Is that why you came? To collect the bracelet?"

Now that he was here, Jefferson couldn't think of how to say what needed saying. He'd had hours on his private jet to rehearse this little speech. To sketch out exactly his plan of attack.

But standing here, with her scent filling him, her gaze locked on him, all the words but three left him. "I love you."

She blinked and her mouth dropped open.

He laughed at her obvious astonishment. And, god, it felt good to laugh again. For days now, he'd been miserable, trying to tell himself that he didn't need her, when the reality was *all* he needed was her.

"I love you. I know you don't have any reason to believe me. But I've never said those words before, Caitlyn. Not to any woman."

"Oh, god…" She backed up a step, but Jefferson didn't let her go far.

He reached for her, cupping his hands over her shoulders and holding on because he needed to be touching her. "They're too important, those words, to be thrown around easily. If you do, they stop meaning what they should. So I was always careful to never say them."

A sheen of moisture filled her eyes, but she blinked it back, and he was more grateful than he could say. It would kill him to see her cry. To know he'd caused her more pain in any way.

"I didn't even realize the truth myself until I was

home." His thumbs moved over her shoulders, then he slid his hands to the column of her throat and up to cup her face between his palms. "I thought I'd go home and everything would be the way it was. The way it was supposed to be. But you weren't there. And nothing was right. Nothing fit anymore."

"Don't…"

He hurried on, hoping she was hearing him, hoping she could believe him. "I couldn't lose myself in work anymore. It wasn't the same. But it wasn't just missing you running my life, handling crises…it was not having you there every morning. Listening to your voice, hearing you laugh. You've become such a part of my world, Caitlyn, that when you were gone nothing worked anymore."

She pulled in a breath and huffed it out. "Jefferson, don't say this if you don't—"

"I *love* you." He repeated the most important words again to make sure she understood. To make sure she *knew* the truth. "I didn't know I could feel like this. But being with you here, touching you, has made the world right again, Caitlyn. I can't be without you. I don't want to live without you in my life."

One tear fell and then another, and Jefferson smoothed them away gently. "Love me, Caitlyn. Let me love you. And, I swear, I'll never give you reason to cry again."

She laughed now, shortly, helplessly. "I don't know what to do about you."

He grinned and let hope fill him. "Just forgive me for

being an idiot. Give me another chance to show you how much I love you. How much I need you."

"I do love you," she said softly, still staring at him as if she couldn't quite believe this was happening.

"Marry me," he whispered. "Marry me today. Tomorrow."

Nodding, Caitlyn said, "I will. I will marry you. Today. Tomorrow. Always."

She swiped away her tears and looked up at him with enough love in her eyes to keep him warm for a lifetime and more. His heart started beating again and Jefferson went with his instincts.

Pulling her in close, he wrapped his arms around her, rested his chin on top of her head and felt everything around him slide into place.

Caitlyn nestled in close, listened to his heartbeat beneath her ear and smiled to herself. It seemed only right that her dreams had come true at a place called Fantasies.

* * * * *

Don't miss the next
REASON FOR REVENGE *with*
SEDUCED BY THE RICH MAN,
available September 2007
from Silhouette Desire!

Welcome to cowboy country...

Turn the page for a sneak preview of
TEXAS BABY
by
Kathleen O'Brien
An exciting new title from Harlequin Superromance
for everyone who loves stories about the West.

Harlequin Superromance—
Where life and love weave together in
emotional and unforgettable ways.

CHAPTER ONE

CHASE TRANSFERRED his gaze to the road and identified a foreign spot on the horizon. A car. Almost half a mile away, where the straight, tree-lined drive met the public road. He could tell it was coming too fast, but judging the speed of a vehicle moving straight toward you was tricky.

It wasn't until it was about two hundred yards away that he realized the driver must be drunk…or crazy. Or both.

The guy was going maybe sixty. On a private drive, out here in ranch country, where kids or horses or tractors or stupid chickens might come darting out any minute, that was criminal. Chase straightened from his comfortable slouch and waved his hands.

"Slow down, you fool," he called out. He took the porch steps quickly and began walking fast down the driveway.

The car veered oddly, from one lane to another, then up onto the slight rise of the thick green spring grass. It just barely missed the fence.

"Slow down, damn it!"

He couldn't see the driver, and he didn't recognize this automobile. It was small and old and couldn't have cost much, even when it was new. It was probably white, but now it needed either a wash or a new paint job or both.

"Damn it, what's wrong with you?"

At the last minute, he had to jump away, because the idiot behind the wheel clearly wasn't going to turn to avoid a collision. He couldn't believe it. The car kept coming, finally slowing a little, but it was too late.

Still going about thirty miles an hour, it slammed into the large, white-brick pillar that marked the front boundaries of the house. The pillar wasn't going to give an inch, so the car had to. The front end folded up like a paper fan.

It seemed to take forever for the car to settle, as if the trauma happened in slow motion, reverberating from the front to the back of the car in ripples of destruction. The front windshield suddenly seemed to ice over with lethal bits of glassy frost. Then the side windows exploded.

The front driver's door wrenched open, as if the car wanted to expel its contents. Metal buckled hideously. Small pieces, like hubcaps and mirrors, skipped and ricocheted insanely across the oyster-shell driveway.

Finally, everything was still. Into the silence, a plume of steam shot up like a geyser, smelling of rust and heat. Its snakelike hiss almost smothered the low, agonized moan of the driver.

Chase's anger had disappeared. He didn't feel anything but a dull sense of disbelief. Things like this didn't happen in real life. Not in his life. Maybe the sun had actually put him to sleep….

But he was already kneeling beside the car. The

driver was a woman. The frosty glass-ice of the windshield was dotted with small flecks of blood. She must have hit it with her head, because just below her hairline a red liquid was seeping out. He touched it. He tried to wipe it away before it reached her eyebrow, though, of course, that made no sense at all. Her eyes were shut.

Was she conscious? Did he dare move her? Her dress was covered in glass and the metal of the car was sticking out lethally in all the wrong places.

Then he remembered, with an intense relief, that every good medical man in the county was here, just behind the house, drinking his champagne. He found his phone and paged Trent.

The woman moaned again.

Alive, then. Thank God for that.

He saw Trent coming toward him, starting out at a lope, but quickly switching to a full run.

"Get Dr. Marchant," Chase called. "Don't bother with 9-1-1."

Trent didn't take long to assess the situation. A fraction of a second, and he began pulling out his cell phone and running toward the house.

The yelling seemed to have roused the woman. She opened her eyes. They were blue and clouded with pain and confusion.

"Chase," she said.

His breath stalled. His head pulled back. "What?"

Her only answer was another moan, and he wondered if he had imagined the word. He reached around her and put his arm behind her shoulders. She was tiny. Probably petite by nature, but surely way too thin. He could feel her shoulder blades pushing against her skin, as fragile as the wishbone in a turkey.

She seemed to have passed out, so he put his other arm under her knees and lifted her out. He tried to avoid the jagged metal, but her skirt caught on a piece and the tearing sound seemed to wake her again.

"No," she said. "Please."

"I'm just trying to help," he said. "It's going to be all right."

She seemed profoundly distressed. She wriggled in his arms, and she was so weak, like a broken bird. It made him feel too big and brutish. And intrusive. As if touching her this way, his bare hands against the warm skin behind her knees, were somehow a transgression.

He wished he could be more delicate. But he smelled gasoline and he knew it wasn't safe to leave her here.

Finally he heard the sound of voices, as guests began to run around the side of the house, alerted by Trent. Dr. Marchant was at the front, racing toward them as if he were forty instead of seventy. Susannah was right behind him, her green dress floating around her trim legs.

"Please," the woman in his arms murmured again. She looked at him, the expression in her blue eyes lost and bewildered. He wondered if she might be on drugs. Hitting her head on the windshield might account for this unfocused, glazed look, but it couldn't explain the crazy driving.

"Please, put me down. Susannah… The wedding…"

Chase's arms tightened instinctively and he froze in

his tracks. She whimpered, and he realized he might be hurting her. "Say that again?"

"The wedding. I have to stop it."

* * * * *

Be sure to look for TEXAS BABY,
available September 11, 2007,
as well as other fantastic Superromance titles
available in September.

Welcome to Cowboy Country...

TEXAS BABY

by *Kathleen O'Brien*

#1441

Chase Clayton doesn't know what to think.
A beautiful stranger has just crashed his
engagement party, demanding that he not
marry because she's pregnant with his baby.
But the kicker is—he's never seen her before.

Look for TEXAS BABY and other fantastic
Superromance titles on sale September 2007.

Available wherever books are sold.

**Where life and love weave together
in emotional and unforgettable ways.**

REQUEST YOUR FREE BOOKS!

2 FREE NOVELS PLUS 2 FREE GIFTS!

Silhouette®

Desire®

Passionate, Powerful, Provocative!

SDES07

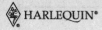
Third time's a charm.

Texas summers. Charlie Morrison.
Jasmine Boudreaux has always connected
the two. Her relationship with Charlie
begins and ends in high school. Twenty
years later it begins again—and ends again.
Now fate has stepped in one more time—
will Jazzy and Charlie finally give in to
the love they've shared all this time?

Look for

Summer After Summer
by
Ann DeFee

Available September
wherever books are sold.